Whisper of Darkness

Legends of Destiny Volume Three

by ACHIEVER OF THE YEAR LINKEDIN AND TOWN HALL
EY NOMINEE ENTREPRENEUR OF THE YEAR
GRAND HOMAGE LYS DIVERSITY
WORLD'S TOP100 DOCTORS
CREA GLOBAL AWARD

Dr. BAK NGUYEN, DMD

&

by PRODIGY
WILLIAM BAK

TO ALL DREAMING AND LOOKING TO MAKE IT REAL

by Dr. BAK NGUYEN & WILLIAM BAK

ISBN: 978-1-998750-24-5

Published by: Dr. BAK PUBLISHING COMPANY
Dr.BAK 0135

Whisper of Darkness

Legends of Destiny Volume Three

by Dr. BAK NGUYEN & WILLIAM BAK

Prologue

Epilogue

BY Dr. BAK NGUYEN & WILLIAM BAK

DISCLAIMER

ABOUT THE CO-AUTHORS

From Canada, **Dr. BAK NGUYEN** is making waves in the dental industry through his company Mdex & Co, his organization, The Alphas, and his books. Dr. Bak has been recognized for his exceptional achievements, including being nominated for the Ernst and Young Entrepreneur of the Year award, receiving the Grand Homage Lys Diversity award, and being named the LinkedIn & TownHall Achiever of the Year and one of the Top 100 Doctors in 2021. His recent accomplishment includes making it to the CREA Global Award list in 2023. He is the first dentist ever to make that list, in 2022, Bill Gates and Sir Richard Branson were part of that list.

In addition to his successful dental career, Dr. Bak is an accomplished author and motivational speaker. He holds several world records for his prolific writing, having written an impressive 120 books in just five years. He has written extensively on topics such as entrepreneurship, leadership, the quest for identity, dentistry and medicine, parenting, children's books, and philosophy. Dr. Bak's passion for sharing knowledge and empowering others led him to establish the international collaborative initiative called THE ALPHAS, aimed at supporting entrepreneurs and doctors during challenging times like the pandemic and economic depression.

Dr. Bak's influence extends beyond his professional endeavours. He co-founded Emotive World Incorporated in 2016, a tech research company focused on utilizing technology to enhance happiness and sharing. Their flagship project, U.A.X., combines the latest advancements in artificial intelligence and techniques from the movie industry to revolutionize the book industry and improve continuing education. By 2023, he is leading the advancement of book writing and audiobook through AI.

With his remarkable achievements, Dr. Nguyen has gained recognition from the international and diplomatic community, sparking global discussions on the well-being and future of the health profession. He actively encourages healthcare professionals to share their experiences and thoughts, emphasizing the importance of unity and collaboration in overcoming challenges.

Dr. Bak's multifaceted persona is described in his own words: a dentist by circumstances, an entrepreneur by nature, and a communicator by passion. His contributions have earned him acknowledgments from the Canadian Parliament and the Canadian Senate, further solidifying his impact and influence.

From Canada, **William Bak**, is a 13 years old prodigy. At the age of 8 years old, he co-wrote a series of chicken books with his dad, Dr. Bak. Together, they are changing the world, one mind at a time, writing books for kids. So far, they have 40 books together and one solo.

He co-wrote the 11 chicken books in ENGLISH and then, had to translate his own books in FRENCH. This is how he has 22 chicken books. William also co-wrote 2 parenting books with his dad, Dr. Bak, the trilogy of THE BOOK OF LEGENDS, THE RISE OF LEGENDS vol.1. 2 Vaccine books (French and English), TIMING, William's first Apollo Protocol book. Lately, William has also written his first book solo at the age of 11, PAPA, J'SUIS PAS CON, HOW TO WRITE 2 BOOKS IN 10 DAYS, and the LEGENDS OF DESTINY, volumes one to four. As well as the trilogy of PAPALAND.

To promote his books, William embraced the stage for the first time in 2019 talking to a crowd of 300+ people. Since he has appeared in many videos to talk about his books and upcoming projects.

In the midst of COVID, he got bored and started his YOUTUBE CHANNEL : GAMEBAK, reviewing video games.
By the end of 2020, he has joined THE ALPHAS as the youngest anchor of the upcoming world project COVIDCONOMICS in which he will give his perspective and host the opinions of his generation.

> "I will show you. I won't force you. But I won't wait for you."
> - William Bak and Dr. Bak

Writing with his Dad, William holds world records to be officialized:

- The youngest author writing in 2 languages
- Co-author of 8 books within a month
- The first kid to have written 20 children's books
- The child to have written his first solo book in 9 days
- The first child to have co-written 43 books by the age of 13

Adrian

ANGEL LORD

LEGENDS
OF
DESTINY

Prologue

by Dr. BAK NGUYEN

This is the tale of Adrian, a celestial warrior whose valour and skill in battle had garnered him a legendary reputation amongst the angels. Along his celestial journey, he had faced countless adversaries, yet none compared to the enigmatic Barakiel.

Barakiel, once a steadfast comrade who fought alongside Adrian and their fellow angels, had undergone a mysterious transformation, succumbing to the allure of darkness and betrayal. Adrian was entrusted with the daunting task of bringing Barakiel to Heaven's justice.

Barakiel had cunning and power at his disposal, bolstered by a legion of smaller gods and titans who had submitted to him, seeking to avoid being devoured by the insatiable Kal, the Old God of Fire.

Their fateful confrontation unfolded in a desolate wasteland, concealed from the watchful eyes of the celestial realm. Adrian approached Barakiel, his sword held high, a symbol of his unwavering resolve. A malicious smirk twisted Barakiel's face as he stood his ground, revelling in his newfound allegiance to the darkness. Do you truly believe you can prevail against me, Adrian? He taunted, his voice dripping with malice.

Undeterred, Adrian lunged forward, silent determination radiating from his being. His sword shimmered in the dim light. As Barakiel retaliated, unleashing a surge of dark energy. Adrian's agility proved to be his advantage as he deftly evaded the attack, swiftly redirecting his blade toward Barakiel's head.

Barakiel, empowered by his alliance with the gods and titans, effortlessly parried Adrian's assault. His own sword hummed with malevolent energy, a testament to the dark forces at his command. The clash of their blades reverberated through the night, a resounding echo of their equal skill and unyielding resolve.

Time stretched on as the battle raged, neither combatant gaining a decisive advantage. Adrian and Barakiel pushed each other to their limits, locked in an unyielding struggle of celestial might and cunning. As the hours wore on, Adrian's strength began to wane. Though he fought valiantly, pouring every ounce of his being into the conflict, the limits of his endurance became apparent.

The gods and titans who had aligned themselves with Barakiel bolstered his power, making the battle, even more, gruelling for Adrian. Seizing the opportune moment, Barakiel struck with precision, his sword cleaving through Adrian's armour, inflicting a deep and agonizing wound. Adrian cried out in anguish, his vigour faltering as the pain coursed through his celestial essence.

Yet just as hope seemed to dwindle, a contingent of angels appeared on the horizon. News of Adrian's peril had reached their ears, propelling them to rush to his aid. They were accompanied by celestial beings who had refused to submit to Barakiel's dark influence, standing against the smaller gods and titans that had once bowed before him.

United in purpose, the angels and their allies confronted Barakiel and the formidable forces he had gathered. Their swords blazed with celestial light, illuminating the darkness that surrounded them. Even the combined might of the gods and titans proved futile against the unwavering determination and unity of the celestial warriors. Victory ultimately belonged to the angels and their newfound allies. Barakiel was defeated and the smaller gods and titans were scattered, their arrogance humbled.

Though wounded, Adrian survived, his life preserved by the timely arrival and unwavering support of his brethren. He approached his defeated old comrade and open his mouth to absorb all of Barakiel's essence. That revived Adrian, but also was a horror show of strength that scared all of the angels, gods, and titans presented. Adrian was now the new ruler to be feared.

However, his triumph was overshadowed by news of an even greater menace on the horizon: Kal, the god of fire, weary of the angels' interference, descended upon the heavens. Accompanied by his dwindling army of demons, Kal sought to assert his dominance over the celestial realm. Recognizing the urgent need for unity, the angels rallied their forces, forging an unbreakable alliance with the celestial beings who had defied Barakiel and the smaller gods. Together, they prepared for the imminent battle, fully aware of the formidable challenge that awaited them.

The heavens trembled as Kal, the god of fire, advanced with his remaining forces, his once mighty army of demons now joined by the desperate and subservient smaller gods and titans. The atmosphere crackled with the intensity of their malevolence, threatening to engulf the celestial realm in flames.

Adrian, though wounded from his previous encounter, stood at the forefront of the angelic host. His determination burned brighter than ever as he assumed a position of leadership, his experience and unwavering resolve guiding their every move. Days bled into nights as the celestial battlefield became a cauldron of chaos and fury.

The angels, bolstered by their newfound allies, fought with unyielding courage and a shared sense of purpose. Swords clashed, celestial energy crackled, and divine powers clashed with the destructive might of the gods and titans. Adrian, fuelled by his unwavering conviction, led the charge against Kal, engaging the god of fire in a titanic clash that shook the heavens. As the battle raged on, the celestial warriors pushed back against Kal's forces with unwavering determination.

The smaller gods and titans, once aligned with Barakiel, now faced the consequences of their ill-fated choice. Some, filled with remorse, turned against their former master, lending their strength to the angel's cause. Adrian, his wounds throbbing with pain, summoned his remaining strength and unleashed a devastating assault on Kal. His blade shimmered with celestial light as he struck with unerring precision aiming for the heart of the God of Fire.

Kal found himself facing the consequences of his tyranny. Adrian's sword pierced through the veil of Kal's defences, plunging deep into the God of Fire's chest. A searing roar of pain erupted from Kal's lips as he recoiled, his forces faltering in the face of his vulnerability.

Kal burst from his wounds. The fire of his blood covered Adrian who caught in fire, one that even his angelic energy could not protect him from. His blue energy melted under the immense heat of Kal's blood, mixing fragments of lighting of red and blue. Adrian fell to the ground.

Kal screamed his pain. For the first time in his life, the god of fire could see the eventuality of his demise, him, the almighty god of fire. He fled the battlefield, leaving all of his minions to their own fate. He ran to find refuge deep in the dark canvas of the unlightened cosmos. This was too close. Just when he thought that he was safe, he bumped into Odin, the calm god of stone. Odin was huge, calm and of a kind heart. He was no threat to Kal. Just when Kal pushed him out of his way, Odin seized Kal and sat on him. "This force of nature has caused too much destruction already." Odin sat on a wounded Kal and fell asleep for 3000 years.

The heavens echoed with the triumphant cries of the angels and their allies as they emerged victorious from the harrowing battle. But the victory came at a great cost. Many valiant angels and celestial beings had fallen, their sacrifices forever etched into the tapestry of the heavens. Adrian, weakened and battered, collapsed onto the scarred battlefield, his strength waning. Yet, even in his vulnerable state, Adrian understood the profound significance of their triumph.

The forces of darkness had been repelled and the celestial realm had been preserved. With the fallen warriors honoured and mourned, the angels vowed to continue their eternal duty of safeguarding the heavens. In the aftermath of the battle, as the echoes of conflict subsided, the celestial beings turned their attention to healing and restoration.

Adrian, embraced by the celestial light, felt the warm currents of rejuvenation course through his celestial essence. His wounds slowly closed, leaving behind marks of resilience and valour. As he rose from the battlefield, a renewed sense of purpose burned within Adrian's heart. Guided by his unwavering resolve, he assumed a position of leadership amongst the angels, inspiring them to rise above their losses and continue their sacred duty, to balance the forces of the Universe.

But Adrian was not the same anymore. His once blue energy was now a mix of blue and red. With the fire of Kal still burning inside of him, sometimes through his body and healed wounds, reinforced his heart as Adrian became a cold ruler, supreme lord of the angels.

From his face-off with Barakiel, he learned to stay away from the corruption of power. From that day on, that became his no prisoners and no mercy policy. In his eyes, one is either good or bad, only corruption lies in between. From the part of Kal burning inside of him, Adrian became cold to hide his continuous burning pain. That pain became a part of him. Ironically, Adrian, whose sole desire was to remain pure, as he fought and triumphed over Kal, his victory corrupted his essence forever. Adrian remains a good ruler, one defending justice, blind justice, and one without emotion or mercy. Adrian became the supreme angel lord.

Adrian's guidance, the angels and their celestial allies rebuilt their ranks, their unity stronger than ever before. Together, they stood as guardians of the heavens, a beacon of hope, and defenders of the celestial realm. As the celestial warriors embraced their renewed purpose, word of their resounding victory and the remarkable restoration of their fallen comrades spread throughout the celestial realms.

Angels from far and wide flocked to their ranks, drawn by the tales of valour and the promise of a united front against the forces of darkness. Under Adrian's leadership, the celestial army underwent rigorous training and preparation. They honed their celestial powers, refining their combat techniques, and deepening their understanding of the intricate web that interconnected the celestial realms. But not all angels agreed with Adrian's black or white vision of the universe. Some Angels fled alone. Others organized into a new dissident fraction that Heaven labelled the Dark Angels, those no more in the light of Heaven.

This is how the Angels, fulfilling their purpose which Ethem, the primal force, created them for, also commenced inner fighting, slowly disturbing the fabric of creation.

This is **Whisper of Darkness**, the third volume of **Legends of Destiny**.

Chapter 1
Echoes of the Past

by Dr. BAK NGUYEN AND WILLIAM BAK

The moon cast an eerie glow over the desolate landscape as Ethel and Adoel found themselves ensnared in the clutches of Hasdielle, the enigmatic Dark Angel, the one plagued with a cruel reputation and openly defying the order of Heaven.

A bone-chilling wind whispered through the trees, carrying with it a sense of impending doom. Ethel's heart pounded in her chest as she witnessed the torment inflicted upon Adoel, her dear friend and companion. The sharp scent of burning feathers hung heavy in the air, mingling with the metallic tang of blood.

Adoel, once a pillar of strength and grace, now trembled in agony as Hasdielle burned part of her wings. The smell of burning feathers and flesh etched the atmosphere. Ethel could hardly bear to watch, her eyes transfixed by the cruel dance of shadows cast upon the cold, stone walls of their prison. Each agonized cry that escaped Adoel's lips pierced Ethel's soul.

As the torment unfolded before her, Ethel could feel her own spirit falter, a knot of fear coiling within her stomach. The malevolence emanating from Hasdielle was suffocating and overwhelming. The darkness that consumed Hasdielle was a void that hungered for chaos and destruction, a presence that defied comprehension, beyond the boundaries of morality and reason.

Ethel's hands trembled, her wings quivering with a mixture of fear and fury. She yearned to rush to Adoel's aid, to break free from the clutches of their captor and unleash her celestial powers upon Hasdielle. But the weight of her own powerlessness pressed upon her, holding her captive as effectively as the chains that bound her. Hasdielle, laughing at such a futile attempt.

Time seemed to stretch, each moment an eternity of torment as Ethel bore witness to the unspeakable acts committed in the shadow of darkness. Adoel's once vibrant wings, radiant with divine light, now hung limp and tattered, stripped of their former glory. It was a desecration of everything they held sacred, a sacrilege against the very essence of their celestial existence.

Amidst the chaos, a flicker of hope emerged. Anak and Charoum, two of heaven's guardians, descended with a thunderous crash. Ethel's heart leaped with fragile hope as she saw the fury burning in their eyes. They unleashed a symphony of righteous fury, their weapons flashing with blinding brilliance. The clash of steel and the echoes of celestial power reverberated through the air, creating a tempestuous symphony of chaos and defiance.

In a final, thunderous blow, Anak and Charoum shattered the chains that held Ethel captive. Free at last, she rushed to Adoel's side, cradling her in her trembling arms. Her gaze met hers, filled with gratitude and pain. Ethel's tears mingled with her blood as they rushed back to Heaven.

As they made their escape, a haunting melody lingered in the air, the lament of their fallen comrades and the testament to the horrors they had endured. The path ahead was treacherous and uncertain, but Ethel's resolve burned brighter than ever. She refused to let the darkness consume her, for within her heart, a flicker of divine light remained.

The moon, once a source of gentle illumination, now seemed to conspire with the shadows, casting sinister shapes upon the rugged terrain. Ethel's wings fluttered nervously, their pristine feathers marred by the stains of Adoel's blood. The world around them appeared distorted, as if reality itself had been warped by the malevolence they had witnessed.

Each step forward was weighed down by the weight of their recent trauma. Ethel's mind replayed the horrific scenes over and over, the cries of agony echoing in her ears. Her body trembled, not just from the chill in the air, but from the bone-deep fear that threatened to consume her. She couldn't shake the feeling that Hasdielle's malevolence still clung to her, a suffocating presence that lingered in the recesses of her mind.

Adoel, weakened but resilient, leaned on Ethel for support. She could feel her pain radiating through their connection, a constant reminder of the atrocities they had endured. Yet, there was a flicker of determination in her eyes, a testament to her unyielding spirit. Together, they pressed on, their footsteps resounding with the rhythm of defiance.

The landscape morphed into a twisted labyrinth, trees gnarled and twisted like the skeletal remains of forgotten souls. Ethel couldn't shake the feeling that unseen eyes watched their every move, lurking within the shadows, waiting for a moment of weakness to strike. The wind whispered sinister secrets, its voice carrying the weight of untold tragedies. Her only consolation was the sight of the 2 guardians of Heaven opening the march in front of her, them too, trembling discreetly.

Fear clung to them like a second skin, prickling their senses and sending shivers down their spines. They were but mortals traversing a realm of nightmares, their ethereal essence no match for the horrors that lurked in the shadows. Yet, they pressed forward, driven by a glimmer of hope and a determination to face their demons head-on.

As they emerged from the labyrinthine woods, a sense of relief washed over them. The moon cast a pale glow upon a desolate landscape, barren and devoid of life. It was a stark reminder of the battles yet to be fought, of the darkness that still threatened to consume them all.

In the distance, a mournful howl pierced the silence, sending a chill down their spines. As the moon reached its zenith, casting an ethereal glow upon their path, Ethel's heart swelled with newfound courage. With a determined glint in her eyes, Ethel led Adoel onward, their footsteps resolute and purposeful. The night seemed to hold its breath, as if the very fabric of reality quivered in anticipation of the battle to come.

The spectre of Hasdielle's cruelty loomed over them, a constant reminder of the darkness that threatened to consume their world. Even as the light of day and the warmth of Heaven welcomed them back.

This is **Whisper of Darkness**, the third volume of **Legends of Destiny**.

Chapter 2
Bitter Taste

by Dr. BAK NGUYEN AND WILLIAM BAK

Years after her traumatic walk in the forest of shadow, Ethel still had to fight for a reputation amongst the Angel. She is pretty and adored by many, but that does not impress the Council of Angels and even less, the Angel Lord who seems to be cold to any beauty or pleasure. Ever since, Ethel enrolled in every mission she could qualify for, often bringing with Eto, the small and weak angel. They got assigned a recognition mission to find a deserter, Kohël, now named Dalo, the God of the Wind.

The air grew heavy with an ominous stillness as Ethel and Eto embarked on their mission to find Kohel. The moon, shrouded behind thick clouds, cast fleeting glimmers of light that danced eerily on the forest floor. It was a too-familiar scenery and ambiance for Ethel. Whispers of unseen creatures echoed through the dense foliage, sending shivers down their spines.

Ethel's heart raced as they ventured deeper into the labyrinthine forest, the path before them obscured by gnarled branches and tangled undergrowth. A chilling wind whistled through the trees, carrying with it a haunting melody that seemed to echo the anguish of lost souls. Long ago, she was tangled in a similar path and yet, it still haunted her.

The mission held more than just the promise of a celestial task; it was an opportunity for Ethel to prove herself to the Council of angels once and for all. The weight of their expectations bore down upon her, mingling with her own self-doubt. She yearned to show her worth, to be acknowledged as more than a mere angel messenger. Eto, driven by his desire to impress Ethel, followed her with unwavering determination.

Their journey took them deeper into the heart of the enchanted forest, where twisted branches reached out like skeletal fingers, grasping at their fleeting hope. Ethel's senses sharpened, each rustle of leaves and hushed whisper erecting their feathers toward the sky. She couldn't shake the feeling of being watched, of unseen eyes studying their every move.

Unbeknownst to Ethel and Eto, Adrian, the stoic leader of the council, had sent two sentinels, Arakiba and Barrattiel, on the same mission. Not quite. They were sent to bring back Kohël while Ethel and Ito were expected to bring news of the deserter. As Ethel and Eto ventured deeper into the forest, the sense of being hunted intensified, the forest itself conspiring against them. A cold sweat broke out on Ethel's brow as a fleeting glimpse of movement caught her eye. She turned, her heart pounding in her chest, only to find emptiness staring back at her. The forest seemed to twist and contort, its very essence morphing into a macabre dance of illusions.

Their path led them to a clearing bathed in an otherworldly glow. A sense of foreboding washed over them, the realization that they had stumbled upon a place where the boundaries between realms blurred. It was in that moment, when the darkness threatened to consume them, that Ethel felt a presence. She turned, her gaze meeting Eto's, and together they saw the silhouettes of Arakiba and Barrattiel emerge from the shadows.

An unspoken understanding passed between Ethel and Eto. They would face this challenge head-on, their determination unyielding. No way to let the sentinels rob them of their prize this time.

The forest itself seemed to hold its breath, waiting for the clash of celestial forces. Arakiba and Barrattiel approached with measured steps, their movements as calculated as the beating of a heart. Their eyes, hidden in the shadows, bore an intensity that sent a chill down Ethel's spine. The air crackled with anticipation, each heartbeat echoing like a death knell.

As the two pairs of warriors locked eyes, a silent exchange passed between them—a mutual understanding of the stakes at hand. There was no room for hesitation, no time for mercy. Survival hung in the balance, and only one would emerge victorious.

Without warning, the forest erupted in a tempest of chaos. Ethel lunged forward, her blade slashing through the air with blinding speed. She clashed with Arakiba. Eto was left to face Barrattiel. That was not even a close match. The clash of their weapons reverberated through the forest, creating a cacophony of sound that mingled with the howling wind.

The Sentinels made very little case of the two angel messengers, dismissing them without even trying. On her behind, Ethel refused to give up. She channelled her determination, her desire to prove herself, and pressed forward. Her strikes grew more fierce, more precise, as she sought to exploit any opening. Beside her, Eto followed with the best, his everything. That did not make a dent.

Out of options and out of resources, Ethel laid her last weapon. With a surge of energy, Ethel made a split-second decision. She called upon the power within, summoning a burst of celestial light that enveloped her and Eto. The blinding radiance acted as a shield, a temporary respite from the relentless onslaught.

As the light dissipated, Ethel and Eto seized the opportunity to retreat, their retreat a strategic move to regroup and plan their next move. They vanished into the depths of the forest, leaving behind a battlefield ravaged by their clash. At least, that way, they will keep face and still be ahead of the sentinel. They rushed back into the depth of the forest, exactly where, a moment ago, they got bone-chilling feelings.

This is 𝔚𝔥𝔦𝔰𝔭𝔢𝔯 𝔬𝔣 𝔇𝔞𝔯𝔨𝔫𝔢𝔰𝔰, the third volume of 𝔏𝔢𝔤𝔢𝔫𝔡𝔰 𝔬𝔣 𝔇𝔢𝔰𝔱𝔦𝔫𝔶.

Chapter 3
The Angel Lake

by Dr. BAK NGUYEN AND WILLIAM BAK

Ethel and Eto, with their bodies still trembling with a potent mix of fear and determination, pushed deeper into the foreboding expanse of the Forest of Shadows. Every rustle of the dense foliage seemed to whisper sinister secrets. Their pursuers, the relentless sentinel angels, were relentless in their chase.

Fate intervened, granting them a sliver of hope amidst the encroaching darkness. By some stroke of luck, the duo stumbled upon a small clearing adorned with an otherworldly blue glow. A massive lake, its surface glistening with enchanting magic, sprawled out before them. Ethel's heart skipped a beat as she recalled the ancient myths and legends passed down through celestial lore—a tale of a sacred blue lake where the primal force, Ethem, had imbued its power to create angels and archangels. Whispers of the lake's ability to heal and amplify celestial beings had reverberated through generations.

- What in the celestial realms... started Eto?
- It's been said, started Ethel, that Ethem created the first Archangels from a blue magical lake. This could be it!
- And what good will that do for us, demanded Eto, confused.
- Well, legends say, continue Ethel, that the lake has the power to heal   any wounded angels and even to boost angelic power. I don't know if that is true, but that is what the legend says.
- Well, reprises Eto, there is only one way to know for sure.

Eto, very confident, approached the edge of the mysterious lake. His intent was to taste the fabled mystical waters, to witness firsthand the power they held. Yet, before his desire could be sated, a sudden splash engulfed him, leaving him drenched from head to toe. Startled, he whirled around to face the source of the disturbance.

Amidst the glimmering blue depths of the lake stood Kohël, the very angel deserter they had tirelessly pursued. Eto's eyes narrowed, his determination reigniting as he lunged forward, attempting to seize Kohël. But the agile renegade slipped away with the swiftness of the wind, leaving Eto grasping at thin air.

- Not again, screamed Eto, gritting his teeth, he's always one step ahead!
- That's him, that's Kohël! Don't let him escape, shouted Ethel, raising her sword, voice firm! We have to capture him this time!

Emerging from the shimmering depths, amidst the ethereal blue, stood Kohël—the very angel deserter they had relentlessly pursued. Eto lunged forward, fuelled by a surge of adrenaline, desperately attempting to seize Kohël and bring an end to this seemingly eternal chase. However, the renegade's agility matched his elusiveness, slipping away from Eto's grasp with the swiftness of the wind. Eto's fervent pursuit was abruptly halted as he stumbled, his ankle twisting beneath him, sending him crashing to the forest floor in a whirlwind of agony.

Undeterred by her companion's misfortune, Ethel drew her gleaming sword, its silver surface gleaming with determination. She refused to let this relentless chase continue unabated, steadfast in her belief that she could outmaneuver the elusive Kohël. Confidence pulsated through her veins as she analyzed his tactics, convinced that she had unraveled his evasive maneuvers.

- I won't let you slip away, Kohël, shout Ethel, focused, determined! Your treachery ends now!

Kohël, however, had other plans. Sensing an opportunity, he enticed Ethel closer, his voice carrying a seductive charm.

- My, my, sweet little child, started Kohël smirking at Ethel. So persistent, aren't we? Come, chase me if you dare.

Ethel, drawn into the dangerous pursuit of Kohël's ever-shifting shadow, couldn't resist the challenge. Her eyes gleamed with determination as she followed him, her movements agile yet cautious. Kohël was a renegade driven by chaos, guided by an unpredictable grace that defied any attempts at prediction. Ethel's assumptions crumbled before her eyes as she realized the futility of her pursuit. A growing sense of frustration welled within her, threatening to consume her resolve.

- You won't elude me this time, Kohël, said Ethel, out of breath! I know your tricks!

But Kohël's unpredictable grace proved formidable. Ethel's pursuit grew more frenzied, her steps quickening, yet Kohël always managed to stay a tantalizing distance ahead.

- Oh, teased Kohël, you're quite the graceful one, but can you keep up?

Suddenly, a misstep. Ethel lost her footing, and the ground gave way beneath her, sending her tumbling into the cool embrace of the magical waters. As Ethel fought against the currents, trying to regain her composure, Kohël approached, a wicked smile on his face. He held all the cards now, and he knew it.

- How does it feel, my dear, mocked Kohël as he was leaning closer? Powerless and humiliated yet?

- You won't break me, Kohël, answer Ethel, eyes blazing with defiance, her voice sharp despite her predicament... I'll make sure justice prevails.

Unbeknownst to her, Kohël had a profound weakness—one that would unwittingly entangle them further. Drawn to Ethel's radiant beauty, he lured her closer, his ever-shifting shadow becoming an irresistible temptress, drawing her into a treacherous dance. With each step, Ethel's determination blinded her to the looming danger, until finally, she lost her footing and plunged into the cool embrace of the magical waters.

Humiliation mixed with frustration as Ethel resurfaced, her celestial power surging through her being. Determined to seize control of the situation, she summoned a radiant light, hoping to freeze Kohël in his tracks. But the cunning renegade anticipated her move, skillfully maneuvering around her, intercepting the celestial energy with a smirk.

- Nice try, my dear, mocked Kohël, but you'll have to do better than that.

Trapped within a shimmering shell of celestial energy, Ethel found herself immobilized and helpless, her gaze filled with defiance and fury.

- How delightful it is to see you like this, whispered Kohël while leaning very close. I really hope that the Angels will spare your beautiful face as they will punish you for your failure at capturing me. Here's an idea, why don't you save yourself from such pain and come with me. I promise to never hurt that perfect beauty of yours!
- You are such a disgrace, shout Ethel, scandaled and upset.

Kohël approached, a smirk playing upon his lips, his eyes glinting with mischief and triumph. He pressed his lips against Ethel's in a mocking kiss, savouring the taste of her frustration and defeat. In a voice laced with mockery, he whispered words that stung like a thousand barbed arrows, his cruel intent apparent.

- **Cherish this kiss, darling, taunted Kohël, his voice dripping with derision. Your refusal to follow me will haunt you for eternity. I here stand heartbroken... Farewell, my love!**

Ethel seethed with rage and humiliation, her pride wounded by Kohël's mocking words. Trapped within the celestial energy shell, she could do nothing but stew in her emotions, her mind aflame with the burning desire for vengeance.

Meanwhile, Eto, his ankle throbbing with pain, summoned the last remnants of his strength. Limping forward, he attempted to seize Kohël once more, fuelled by a mixture of determination and wounded pride. But as had become the pattern, Eto's efforts were futile against the renegade's unmatched agility. Kohël vanished into the shadows, leaving Eto to push Ethel and her celestial prison into the welcoming waters of the Angel Lake.

Emerging from the lake's depths, both drenched and alone, Ethel and Eto confronted the reality of their elusive quarry slipping away once again. The waters clung to their bodies, a chilling reminder of their failure and the desperate task that lay ahead. Ethel's heart burned with an unwavering desire for retribution.

Eto looked at the lake at shared:

- **Maybe... Maybe the water can heal us, mumbled Eto. We've come this far... it's worth a try.**

- We've been through so much already, raged Ethel. I don't have time for more disappointments.
- We need every advantage we can get, continued Eto, determined, clenching his fists. This lake... it holds the power of Ethem. It could help us.

Ethel hesitates, her gaze shifting from Eto's wounded ankle to the shimmering waters before them. What did they have to lose anyway, Kohël was already far in the wind, with the wind!? She observed quietly Eto lowering himself to the edge of the lake. His hand was trembling as he dips it into the water and brings it to his lips. He takes a tentative sip, hope and anticipation etched on his face.

- Well, asked Ethel after a long silence.
- I don't know, answered Eto, I don't feel any different.

And as he tried to walk on his twisted ankle, the pain extracted from him an even louder pain, one of disappointment and humiliation.

- Let me try, said Ethel. Perhaps it will have a different effect on me.

Eto watched as Ethel approached the lake cautiously, her wounded pride still lingering beneath her determined exterior. She kneeled down, cupping her hands and taking a small sip from the enchanted waters. Nothing…

- I guess, started Eto, that it did not heal your pride either...
- Are you mocking me, angered Ethel, fuelling with rage and frustration?!

This is **Whisper of Darkness**, the third volume of **Legends of Destiny**.

48

Kohël

ERRANT

LEGENDS

Chapter 4
All too familiar

by Dr. BAK NGUYEN AND WILLIAM BAK

Ethel and Eto headed back into the forest, Eto limping with his twisted ankle and Ethel smoking from a wounded pride. Until then, it was just a mission and a challenge to bring back a deserter. Now, it was personal for both of them. For Ethel, it was now her honour at stake and for Eto, he needed a way to regain value in the eyes of Ethel.

It is impossible to catch Kohël, since his power is to be faster than the wind itself, but he surely left a trail behind, one easy to follow. Eto proposed to call the sentinels and to set them in the right direction. That would have completed their mission and they could leave this sinister forest. But Ethel was in no mood to do anyone, any favour. They will catch Kohël and make him pay dearly for his offence.

Eto did not have a say, he followed Ethel into the forest of shadows. It did not take long before the forest of shadow tightened back its grip on these two, with its branches like skeleton fingers, pushing its preys deeper inside of its belly.

They retreated deeper into the heart of the forest, a sense of impending doom hung heavy in the air. The silence that enveloped them was deafening, broken only by the soft rustling of leaves and the distant hoot of an owl. Ethel's heart pounded against her ribcage, her breaths shallow and rapid, as she fought to steady her trembling hands.

Unbeknownst to them, Hasdielle, a malevolent force of darkness, lay in wait. Her presence lurked in the shadows, an unseen predator biding her time. Ethel's instincts screamed at her, warning of an imminent danger, but the source remained elusive.

Suddenly, the tranquillity shattered as a surge of malevolence erupted from the darkness. Eto instinctively stepped forward, his stance protective, as a hooded figure emerged from the veil of night. Hasdielle, adorned in an ebony cloak that seemed to absorb all light, exuded an aura of power that sent shivers down Ethel's spine.

Eto lunged at Hasdielle, his determination to protect Ethel fuelling his every move. But the malevolent force was cunning and swift, effortlessly sidestepping his attack. Ethel watched in horror as Eto's form collided with the unforgiving ground. The impact resonating through the silent forest.

Hasdielle's laughter pierced the stillness, a chilling sound that echoed in Ethel's ears. She watched helplessly as the malevolent force seized Eto, overpowering him with a strength that seemed unnatural. Hasdielle, the dark angel has a special power, to make others feel so small. Ethel's heart raced, torn between her desire to save Eto and the paralyzing fear that held her captive.

Her mind screamed at her to act, to flee, to do something, anything! A suffocating weight pressed upon her chest, its icy grip consuming all of her will. Ethel's legs felt like lead fused with the dirt at her feet. She was trapped, helpless, as Hasdielle taunted her with sadistic delight.

Hasdielle's voice dripped with venom as she taunted Ethel, revelling in her powerlessness and resuscitating past emotions.

She circled Eto, her every movement graceful and predatory, like an invisible serpent ready to strike. Ethel's eyes widened in terror as Hasdielle's dark magic surged, a maleficent energy coiling around her captive comrade.

In a haunting display of power, Hasdielle summoned a scorpion-like creature, its massive form casting long, ominous shadows. The creature's tail writhed with a serpentine agility, its lethal stinger poised to strike. Ethel's voice caught in her throat, her worst nightmares brought to life before her eyes.

With a sickening realization, Ethel understood that Hasdielle intended to extract Eto's essence, draining him of his very life force. She heard about such myths and never thought that anyone could be so cruel... A bone-chilling fear gripped all of her soul. Driven by desperate courage, Ethel mustered every ounce of strength left within her. She fought against the paralyzing fear. With a surge of determination, she took hesitant steps toward Hasdielle and her captive companion, her heart pounding in her ears.

The air crackled with tension as Ethel stood before the malevolent force. Hasdielle's wicked grin widened, her eyes gleaming with sadistic pleasure. Ethel's voice quivered, but she found the courage to speak, her words laced with a desperate plea.

"Release him." Ethel's voice quivered, her plea echoing through the stillness of the forest. Hasdielle's laughter reverberated through the clearing, a haunting symphony of cruelty. "Why should I grant your pleasure, little angel? What do you have to offer in exchange?" Her voice dripped with malice, each word a venomous taunt.

Ethel's breath hitched, her heart pounding against her chest. She knew she had to find a way to save Eto, to break the chains of fear that bound her. "I will spare your life. Two of Heaven's greatest sentinels are closing on us, you don't want this day to be your last! Your malevolence will not go unpunished."

Hasdielle's dark eyes narrowed, her amusement morphing into a flicker of rage. The malevolent force revelled in the fear that clung to Ethel like a suffocating shroud. She circled Ethel, each step exuding a sinister grace, her voice a seductive whisper that sent shivers down Ethel's spine.

"Oh, my dear little one, I can smell your fear, it is intoxicating! Let them come, the more, the merrier..." A mixture of amusement and curiosity flashed across Hasdielle's face. "Very well, little angel," she purred. "Let us dance, and may the shadows consume you."

With those ominous words, Hasdielle released Eto from her grip, allowing him to crumple to the forest floor. He felt on the ground, lifeless. As Ethel and Hasdielle locked eyes, an electric tension filled the air, charged with a potent mix of fear and determination. The forest held its breath, the spirits of the ancient trees whispering their silent prayers for Ethel's success.

With a surge of celestial energy, Ethel summoned her wings, their ethereal glow illuminating the darkness around her. She raised her celestial blade, the weapon pulsating with a radiant light, ready to cut the night in two.

The dance of shadows began, a battle of light against darkness. Ethel moved with a newfound agility, her every strike fuelled by a combination of fear and wounded pride. Hasdielle, caught off guard by Ethel's resilience, met each blow with a chilling ferocity.

Ethel's movements became a blur of determination, her fear transformed into an unwavering resolve. She deflected Hasdielle's attacks with calculated precision, her celestial blade shimmering as it met the malevolent force's dark magic. But Hasdielle is not one to fight fair. She blows and from her mouth, a green fog engulfed Ethel.

Ethel was as good as blind. Her mind pinned and her senses got confused. She heard Hasdielle's sinister laugh close, too close, almost as a whisper. And fear grew back in her veins, pumping harder at each moment. Hasdielle, sensing Ethel's vulnerability, seized the opportunity. She launched a devastating assault, unleashing a torrent of darkness.

As Ethel fought to hold her ground, her mind raced for a solution. She couldn't afford to falter, not a second time. With a surge of desperation, she gave into her instincts: her wings glowing brighter as she summoned a burst of celestial energy. In one swift motion, Ethel unleashed a blinding wave of light, swallowing Hasdielle. That was just light, but it shined throughout the entire forest, catching the attention of Sentinels Arikiba and Barrattiel.

But just as rescue seemed within grasp, a sudden tremor shook the ground beneath them. The forest itself seemed to groan in protest, the trees swaying with an unnatural fury.

2 giant scorpions rose from the dirt. They smelled fear and blood and were summoned from Ethel sweat and tears, drawn to the chaos like a moth to a flame. Ethel's blood ran cold at the sight of them, her fear amplified by the realization that her battle had only just begun.

This is **Whisper of Darkness**, the third volume of **Legends of Destiny**.

Chapter 5
The Battle of Shadows

by Dr. BAK NGUYEN AND WILLIAM BAK

Dread washed over Ethel as she found herself trapped in the sinister presence of two monstrous scorpions. With their venomous stingers poised they moved with an unsettling fluidity. Ethel's heart pounded in her chest, her breath caught in her throat, as she stared into their soulless, black eyes. She knew that survival demanded an act of extraordinary skill and bravery.

Summoning every ounce of her strength, Ethel became a wraith in motion. With a grace that defied the law of gravity, she skillfully evaded the scorpions' lightning-fast attacks. Her body weaved and contorted, narrowly escaping their deadly strikes. The dance of survival became her art, each movement a testament to her will to live.

Yet, as Ethel embraced the shadows, drawing upon her inner strength, a sinister force stirred in the depths of the ancient forest. Unbeknownst to her, her connection to the darkness awakened more than she had bargained for. A colossal oak tree, twisted and gnarled with centuries of malevolence, awoke from its slumber, consumed by an unquenchable rage. It was joined by a horde of smaller tree creatures, their limbs creaking and cracking with a cacophony of ancient fury.

As the tree creature raced, he caught on to one the giant scorpions and stepped on it as if it was dirt, leaving a lifeless corpse behind. This titanesque menace was one of a kind. That did not stir away the other scorpion that still hunting, its claws and tail always at inches of pinning Ethel down for good.

In the blink of an eye, the scorpion was upon her, its pincers snapping shut with a bone-chilling click. Ethel parried with precision and agility, her every movement guided by a combination of instinct and skill. The clash of metal against chitin reverberated through the air, a macabre symphony of life and death.

But before the scorpion could deliver its final strike, the vengeful giant oak tree, its form twisted and mangled, arrived in a thunderous fury. It reached out with its massive limbs, its gnarled branches closing around both Ethel and the scorpion in a vice-like grip. Desperation surged within Ethel as the tree's grip tightened, threatening to crush her. She wriggled and fought, her every fibre screaming for escape. And then, with a deafening crack, the edge of the cliff gave way.

Time seemed to slow as the world spun in a disorienting whirl. Ethel, the scorpion, and the oak tree were suspended in mid-air, their fates entwined as gravity's pull grew ever stronger. The weight of their struggle proved too much for the fragile ground beneath them.

The scorpion, with its unnaturally precise strikes, revealed an eerie intelligence that surpassed mere instinct. Yet, Ethel refused to yield to despair. She delved deeper into her connection with the forest, tapping into the very life force that coursed through its veins. The energy surged within her, intertwining light and darkness in a mesmerizing display. Her eyes closed, she became a conduit of nature's raw power.

In a blinding spectacle, Ethel unleashed a torrential surge of luminous radiance and engulfing shadows. The battleground became a realm of chaos and disorientation as the scorpion and tree creatures were momentarily blinded by the brilliance of her unleashed power. Shadows danced and writhed, embracing the light, only to swallow it once more.

Seizing the opportunity, Ethel fled but arrived at the edge of a brutal cliff, her heart pounding with the urgency of her escape. It was too late to turn back, the Scorpion and the army of trees were closing down on her. She could feel the hot breath of the relentless scorpion behind her, its venomous sting eager to claim her essence. And there, charging with a terrifying vengeance, came the wrathful giant oak tree, its branches reaching out like talons, hungry for revenge.

At the precipice, Ethel stood defiant, her sword raised high in a final act of resistance. The scorpion lunged forward, driven by primal fury, ready to end her life. In a twist of fate, the colossal oak tree arrived just in time, its massive form converging upon them both. The edge of the cliff groaned under the weight of the three combatants, strained beyond its limits. As the ground crumbled beneath them, the abyss beckoned, its darkness yawning wide. The scorpion's final strike was thwarted, frozen in time, as the entire cliff succumbed to the relentless pull of the churning ocean below.

Ethel found herself hurtling through the void, surrounded by a tempest of shattered rock and crashing waves. The horrors of the deep, swallowing ocean loomed before her, its black depths teeming with unknown terrors. Ethel's heart raced as she looked back, only to find the monstrous scorpion and the enraged giant oak tree tumbling alongside her, their twisted forms swallowed by the relentless abyss.

Fear gripped her, but in that moment of desperation, a surge of determination coursed through her veins. She refused to succumb to the watery grave that awaited her. With a firm grip on her sword, she braced herself for what lay ahead.

In the depths of the suffocating ocean, Ethel fought against the relentless pull, her body thrashing in the icy currents. The swirling darkness obscured her vision, disorienting her and filling her lungs with the bitter taste of saltwater. With a surge of determination, she kicked against the suffocating currents, propelling herself upwards towards the faint glimmers of light dancing on the water's surface. Her muscles burned with exhaustion, her body aching from the relentless battle and the merciless grip of the ocean.

At the brink of surrender, her hand broke through the surface, gasping for precious air. She emerged, battered and bruised, but alive. The storm raged on, rain pelting her weary form as she clung to a shard of debris that had once been a part of the cliff.

Ethel's eyes scanned the desolate expanse, searching for any sign of salvation. The dark ocean stretched out before her, unforgiving and treacherous. There was no sight of the scorpion or the oak tree that had chased her to this watery grave. They were consumed by the depths, lost to the abyss.

Though her body screamed for rest, Ethel knew she had to keep going. She mustered every ounce of strength and summoned a reserve of courage from the depths of her being. With a weary stroke, she began swimming towards a distant silhouette on the horizon, hoping it held the promise of safety. Hour after gruelling hour, she battled the relentless waves, her tired limbs pushing against the unyielding resistance. Doubt and fatigue threatened to drag her back into the abyss, but she refused to relent. Her will to survive burned brighter than ever before.

Finally, as her strength waned, she reached the silhouette—a weathered ship, abandoned and left to the mercy of the unforgiving sea. Ethel clung to its hull, her fingers finding purchase on splintered wood, and hauled herself aboard. The ship creaked and groaned beneath her weight, but it offered a sanctuary from the treacherous waters.

Alone on the decaying vessel, Ethel collapsed onto the worn deck, her breath ragged and her body trembling. She had emerged from the horrors of the deep, but scars, both visible and invisible, adorned her spirit. The battle had tested her in ways she could never have imagined, pushing her to the very limits of her strength and resilience.

As she lay there, battered and broken, the realization washed over her—a newfound understanding of her own indomitable spirit. She had faced the embodiment of horror and survived. The shadows had tried to consume her, not once but twice but she had emerged with a flicker of light still burning within her.

Gazing up at the storm-laden sky, Ethel felt a sense of gratitude amidst the chaos. She knew that the path ahead would be fraught with peril, but she also knew that she possessed a strength beyond measure—a strength forged in the crucible of darkness.

As the tempest raged on, Ethel closed her eyes, allowing the rhythmic rocking of the abandoned ship to lull her into a fitful slumber. Dreams of new battles and unknown adventures danced in her mind, whispering of the trials yet to come. She was floating inside a shipwreck surfing the anger of the sea. Her wings were soaked and useless, and her heart was completely drained. She closed her eyes and this time, gave in to Fate.

The storm raged on, the ship creaked and swayed beneath Ethel, a vessel destined to carry her through the uncharted waters of her destiny. The battle of shadows had scarred her, tested her to her bones, and transformed her at her core. But it had not broken her. With each passing moment, Ethel, unconscious, sailed further into the abyss, ready to meet her destiny.

This is **Whisper of Darkness**, the third volume of **Legends of Destiny**.

Barrattiel

SENTINEL

LEGENDS
OF
DESTINY

Chapter 6
The Forbidden Cavern

by Dr. BAK NGUYEN AND WILLIAM BAK

Ethel found herself in a treacherous predicament. Her wings, drenched by the relentless rain, refused to bear her weight, leaving her stranded amidst the tumultuous waves. The desolation of her surroundings mirrored the unease in her heart as she desperately fought to stay afloat, her body succumbing to the relentless pull of the currents.

Suddenly, from the murky depths, a monstrous creature emerged —a nightmarish amalgamation of shark and nightmare. Its cold, soulless eyes fixated on Ethel's vulnerable form, a glimmer of hunger gleaming within them. Fear seized her heart, constricting her breath, as she comprehended the grave danger that loomed before her.

Summoning her dwindling strength, Ethel clutched her sword tightly, the cool touch of the blade providing a fleeting reassurance. With a primal battle cry, she lunged toward the monstrous predator, defying the overwhelming odds stacked against her.

The clash was fierce and unforgiving. Ethel's movements were fuelled by desperation and determination, as she weaved through the water with a dancer's grace. Each stroke of her sword was a testament to her unwavering resolve, aiming for the vulnerable spots on the creature's hulking frame. With a swift and calculated strike, she plunged her blade deep into the creature's flesh, eliciting a guttural roar of pain and fury.

However, the creature's agony only seemed to fuel its rage. In a violent thrash of its gargantuan form, it shattered the remnants of the boat that had kept them afloat, casting Ethel once again into the merciless depths. As the abyss swallowed her, a maelstrom of fear and adrenaline coursed through her veins.

Undeterred by the encroaching darkness, Ethel's survival instincts kicked in. With the agility of a cornered animal, she swam frantically, her senses heightened, aware of the monstrous presence closing in on her from all sides. Just as the jaws of the shark-like beast were poised to ensnare her, she swung her sword with swift precision, the blade slicing through the creature's sensitive snout.

Momentarily stunned, the wounded creature recoiled, allowing Ethel a brief respite. Gasping for air, she struggled to regain her composure amidst the chaotic waters. However, her momentary reprieve was short-lived as the creature retaliated with a powerful thrash of its tail.

The force of the blow sent Ethel spiralling through the dark abyss, her body battered and bruised, consciousness slipping away like a fading ember. As her vision blurred and the weight of her injuries dragged her under, a deep darkness descended, enveloping her in its cold embrace. The world faded to black as Ethel succumbed to the overwhelming forces that conspired against her.

When Ethel regained consciousness, she found herself lying on a desolate, eerie beach, devoid of any signs of life. The air was thick with an unsettling silence, broken only by the distant sounds of the raging ocean. She was alone, stranded on a deserted island.

As Ethel surveyed her surroundings, she felt an eerie presence watching her from the dense forest. Green smoking eyes peered at her with curiosity and suspicion. Reluctant to leave the safety of the beach, Ethel hesitated, sensing a foreboding force at work. However, the sky grew darker, almost violent, unleashing a furious storm upon her. Thunder rumbled ominously, and violent winds threatened to tear her apart. It was like she just upset a God, wounding the Shark-like creature.

Realizing that she had no choice but to seek refuge in the ominous forest, Ethel ran, the wind howling mercilessly around her. Desperate to find shelter, she clung to a towering tree, hoping it would shield her from the relentless onslaught. To her surprise, the tree came to life, its branches wrapping around her, holding her firmly, tenderly.

In the midst of this chaotic moment, Ethel heard a familiar voice crying out for help. She turned her gaze and saw Kohël, desperately clinging to a neighbouring tree that was also struggling against the raging storm. Without a second thought, Ethel reached out her hand, braving the wrath of the tempest, and pulled Kohël to safety.

As the storm subsided, the tree released its hold on Ethel, revealing that it harboured no ill intentions. It was simply responding to the chaotic energy around them. That tree has eyes and mouth, just like those chasing her earlier, but this one seems stranger to what happen inland. Ethel and Kohël keep that incident quiet while talking with their saviour.

- Thank you, started Ethel, her voice filled with gratitude, for coming to our aid. We are forever grateful for your protection.
- Yes, gratitude, added Kohël. We owe you our lives. Your unexpected intervention saved us from certain doom.
- You are welcome, travellers, answer the tree creature. That was not too difficult. Beware, for our current location is far from auspicious.
- What do you mean, demanded Ethel, intrigued and concerned? Where exactly are we?
- We stand upon the edge of the land of the dead, detailed the tree creature, in a much sombre tone, a realm from which no soul has ever returned. It is a place filled with shadows and eternal darkness.
- The land of the dead, repeated Ethel in dismayed? How did we end up in the land of the dead? Is there no way back?
- I'm afraid not, continued the Tree creature. Once you cross this threshold, there is no turning back. The land of the dead holds a grip on all who enter, ensnaring their souls and preventing any escape.
- Tell me, requested Ethel, curiosity piqued, about the boat and the shark that attacked us. Whose domain do they belong to?
- The boat is Charon's, begun the Tree Creature, the ferryman of the dead. He guides souls across the dark waters to the afterlife. The shark, his loyal companion, is a guardian of the realm. Killing it, you just made into an enemy the only means out of this cursed land. Charon will hunt you down. This is his domain!
- So, continued Ethel, by slaying the shark, I have incurred the wrath of Charon. I have become a target, marked for death?
- Unfortunately, concluded the Tree Creature. You are now in grave danger. The ferryman will not rest until he has claimed your soul.
- We must find a way to escape this cursed place, boldly added Kohël, visually shaken by the events. What about flying away once our wings are dry?
- You are in the land of the dead, threw the Tree Creature to Kohl's face. Time stands still here! The winds that would dry your wings are frozen, leaving them perpetually wet and useless. It is a cruel fate, but you are grounded forever!

- No wind, no way to escape... cursed Kohël with frustration. What hope do we have then? Are we destined to be trapped here forever?
- Alas, reprised the Tree Creature, I have no answers to offer. We are all prisoners in this desolate realm.

The three fell into a heavy silence, their hearts burdened by the realization that their escape seemed impossible. The land of the dead held them captive, its grip tightening with every passing moment. As they stood beneath the shadows, the weight of their hopeless situation settled upon them, their future uncertain and bleak.Overwhelmed by despair, Ethel succumbed to her emotions, collapsing to the ground in tears. The weight of their dire circumstances bore down on her, and she couldn't help but feel the hopelessness enveloping them. It seemed as if all paths were closed, leaving them trapped in this desolate realm.

As Ethel wept, the Tree Creature, still under the sway of her charm, attempted to console her. Memories of a long-forgotten myth resurfaced within its ancient consciousness, though it couldn't be certain if the tale held any truth.

- I can't bear the thought of being trapped here forever, wept Ethel. I am too young to die. Is there no way out of this desolate place?
- Please, do not weep, my dear, reassured the Tree Creature, under the sway of Ethel's charm, attempting to console her. There might be a glimmer of hope, a long-forgotten myth that echoes within my ancient consciousness.
- A myth? Please tell me, my friend, begged Ethel, eyes widening with anticipation. If there is a way, I want to know. Tell me majestic Tree, I will be forever in your dept.
- I cannot be certain if this tale holds any truth, continued the Tree Creature with tenderness, but there is a whispered legend of a hidden cavern deep within the heart of this island. It is said to be a place where the souls of the dead vanish, never to resurface.

- A hidden cavern, interrupted Kohël? Could it be a passage, a way to escape the clutches of this wretched realm?
- Don't cut me when I talk, spit the Tree Creature. Turning back its attention to Ethel, it continues. It is not a path to the land of the living, but its true destination remains a mystery. It could hold the key to defying the immutable laws of the land of the dead.

Ethel's eyes widened with a glimmer of hope. Perhaps this mythical cavern held the key to their escape, a chance to defy the immutable laws of the land of the dead. Determination ignited within her, fuelling her resolve to seek out this hidden passage. Yet, as Ethel and Kohël moved towards the cavern, the tree, sensing their intentions, revealed a newfound hostility. Its branches snaked out, attempting to ensnare Ethel and keep her from venturing further.

- Who said that you are forever grateful, said the Tree Creature, very agitated. You are mine, I won't let you go!

Ethel fought back, desperately struggling to break free from its grasp, but it proved to be too overpowering. In her struggle, she dropped her sword, leaving her defenceless. Kohël, who had been concealing himself within the depths of the forest, witnessed the peril Ethel faced. In a daring act, he lunged forward and seized Ethel's fallen blade. With swift precision, he struck the tree's hand, severing the grip it had on her. Together, they escaped the tree's clutches and fled deeper into the heart of the forest, their determination unyielding.

As they ventured further, the atmosphere grew increasingly suffocating. The air was thick with a sense of foreboding, the eerie silence broken only by the distant whispers of lost souls.

Ethel and Kohël pressed on, their footsteps muffled by the dense undergrowth.

Finally, they arrived at the entrance of the hidden cavern, a portal shrouded in darkness. It emanated an otherworldly aura. Hesitation gripped them, for they knew that stepping into this abyss meant forsaking the known and embracing the unknown.

Ethel took a deep breath, her resolve solidifying. She turned to Kohël, her eyes filled with determination. They were prepared to face whatever lay beyond, to defy the very fabric of the land of the dead. They stood at the mouth of the cavern, its yawning darkness swallowing any trace of light that dared to venture inside. Ethel's heart pounded within her chest as she glanced nervously at Kohël, her newfound ally in this treacherous realm. But as the dim light cast eerie shadows across his face, she saw a malevolence lurking in his eyes that sent a chill down her spine.

- **Enter the cavern, commanded Kohël, his voice laced with a sinister undertone.**

Ethel's instincts screamed at her to resist, to fight back against this newfound threat. She mustered her courage and demanded her sword back, hoping to regain her only means of defence. To her horror, Kohël's true colours unveiled themselves, his facade of friendship crumbling away like ancient, weathered stone. He sneered, gripping the sword tightly in his hand, refusing to relinquish it to its rightful owner. A cruel smile danced upon his lips as he revelled in his newfound power.

- **You foolish girl, Kohël hissed, the words dripping with contempt. I will not part with this weapon. It is the key to my survival. Sorry girl, you will have to find your own. Finders, keepers**

Ethel's blood ran cold at his words, her sense of betrayal cutting deeper than any blade. She realized she had no choice. She braced herself for the impending struggle, summoning every ounce of strength within her. But against Kohël's unyielding force, she was no match. He kicked her through the mouth of the cavern, sending her head-first into the dark abyss.

This is **Whisper of Darkness**, the third volume of **Legends of Destiny**.

Chapter 7
A Haunting Reflection

by Dr. BAK NGUYEN AND WILLIAM BAK

The wind howled through the desolate landscape, carrying with it an eerie sense of foreboding. Ethel, her mind burdened with uncertainty, found herself drawn to a secluded cave hidden amidst the jagged rocks. As she cautiously entered, the atmosphere shifted, enveloping her in a chilling embrace. The cave's walls bore ancient markings, etched by long-forgotten hands as if whispering secrets of the past.

A single tree, a stark contrast against the darkness, stood tall in the cave's centre. Its branches, twisted and contorted, reached out like skeletal fingers, seemingly pointing towards a fateful encounter yet to unfold. Ethel's footsteps echoed throughout the hollow space, mingling with the howling wind, as she ventured deeper into the heart of the cavern.

Within the dimly lit cave, the air grew heavy with a palpable sense of dread. Ethel's heart pounded in her chest, a rhythmic reminder of the imminent confrontation that awaited her. And there, amidst the shadows, stood her mysterious and unsettling opponent. A creature that defied categorization, with wings bearing the dual markings of an angel's grace and something far more sinistre.

Their eyes locked in a deadly dance, a silent exchange of intensity and challenge. It was as if time itself had ceased to exist as if the weight of the world hinged on this single moment. Ethel, a mere mortal, stood resolute against her enigmatic adversary, their gazes locking in a relentless struggle of wills.

- Who... what are you, asked Ethel, clenching her fists, determination in her voice?

- I am your deepest fear, whispered the mysterious Creature, her voice echoing with an otherworldly resonance. A reflection of your own twisted destiny.

Without a sword to defend herself, Ethel relied solely on her wits and physical prowess. To her surprise, her opponent held back, delivering calculated blows that seemed almost choreographed. Their movements mirrored each other with uncanny precision as if they were locked in a macabre dance.

- I won't let you defeat me, screamed Ethel, gritting her teeth, defying the odds! I am stronger than my fears!

As the relentless battle unfurled, the air thickened with ominous tension, shrouded in the darkness of impending doom. Ethel's senses heightened, her heart pounding like a war drum within her chest. Her wide, fearful eyes fixated on the menacing glint emanating from her opponent's sword, casting eerie reflections in the dimly lit arena.

A surge of audacity coursed through Ethel's veins, fuelled by desperation and the overwhelming urge to survive. Ignoring the tremors that threatened to betray her resolve, she gathered her remaining strength and launched herself forward, an embodiment of primal determination. With a swift and desperate maneuver, she snatched the enemy's weapon from their grip, her fingers trembling in both anticipation and trepidation.

The blade, a malevolent instrument of destruction, became an extension of Ethel's will. As it sliced through the air, a haunting symphony of dread echoed in its wake. Time seemed to stand still as the metal met flesh with a sickening, bone-chilling thud. Her adversary's anguished cry pierced the air, intertwining with the cacophony of violence that surrounded them.

Yet, Ethel's audacious act of retribution came at a sinister price. A searing, visceral agony surged through her own wounded limb, seeping into the very core of her being. The once potent rush of adrenaline now transformed into a venomous torment, spreading its insidious tendrils throughout her body. The relentless pain threatened to consume her, gnawing at her resolve like a relentless predator.

- **How... commence Ethel, eyes wide with disbelief, why am I feeling your pain?**

In that macabre tableau, the battle unfolded as a twisted dance of agony and desperation. Ethel, now burdened with her own suffering, struggled to maintain her footing, her face contorting in a silent scream. Each breath became a struggle as if the very air she inhaled was laced with the miasma of death itself.

Haunted by her actions, Ethel gazed upon her wounded opponent, their agony mirroring her own. The dim light cast haunting shadows upon their contorted faces, rendering them as grotesque spectres caught in the grip of unyielding terror. With a mixture of trepidation and curiosity, Ethel seized the opportunity. She reached out, pulling back her opponent's hood, revealing the face hidden beneath. A gasp escaped her lips as she gazed upon the visage before her. The left side of the face bore an uncanny resemblance to her own, while the right side was grotesquely disfigured, scarred by an intense burn.

- **No... it can't be, whispered Ethel in horror. That's... that's my face!**

The creature swiftly recovered, pulling her cloak tightly around her form. Her voice carried a mix of urgency and hope.

- Listen to me, threw the creature from a distance, our future is not set in stone! You can still change the path that lies ahead. Do not let fear bind you, bind us into this hideous future.

Fear and realization mingled within Ethel's eyes. She knew that her future self spoke a painful truth. The spectre of losing her beauty, her identity, loomed over her like a dark omen.

- But... continue Ethel with a trembling voice, how can I change something that hasn't happened yet? How can I escape this curse?

Her future self's eyes brimmed with a mixture of sorrow and understanding. She reached out, a gesture of silent empathy. But before she could speak further, Ethel's panic overtook her. With a hasty retreat, she stumbled backward, leaving the cave behind, haunted by the echoes of her own fears.

This is **Whisper of Darkness**, the third volume of **Legends of Destiny**.

LEGENDS

hecate

Chapter 8
The Essence of Shadows

by Dr. BAK NGUYEN AND WILLIAM BAK

The oppressive woods exuded a palpable sense of foreboding, its eerie stillness broken only by the stifling darkness that enveloped every inch of the gnarled trees. The sentinels, Arikiba and Barrattiel stood frozen amidst the encroaching abyss. They were encircled by an army of towering trees, twisted and contorted in grotesque shapes, their branches extending like gnashing claws eager to claim their prey.

Arakiba and Barrattiel, valiant warriors of the sacred realm, locked eyes, a silent understanding passing between them amidst the suffocating silence. They knew they stood against an unknown adversary, a sinister force lurking within the depths of the forest, ready to unleash its wrath upon them. As dread clung to the air like a heavy shroud, a figure emerged from the dense foliage, veiled in shadows that danced and swirled around its form. Hasdielle, with her true identity concealed behind a tenebrous cloak, strode forward with an unsettling grace, their presence exuding an aura of malevolence that sent shivers down the spines of even the bravest warriors.

It was as though Hasdielle, cloaked in darkness, took on the visage of a demon rather than an angelic being. Their every movement seemed to mock the sanctity of their celestial origins, as if they were a renegade spirit, severed from the benevolence that once defined them. Yet, it was this very facade that allowed Hasdielle to approach the tree creatures unscathed, as they were perceived as an entity born from the same macabre realm.

With a voice that echoed through the forest, a haunting whisper that seemed to emerge from the very bowels of the earth,

Hasdielle commanded the attention of the ancient trees. Their words carried a weight of authority, mingled with an undercurrent of twisted malice that resonated with the very essence of the darkened woods. The trees, entangled in their malevolent existence, responded to this call, swaying and creaking in a twisted harmony, as if under the thrall of an unholy conductor.

In the face of this unholy alliance between the enigmatic Hasdielle and the sinister trees, the sentinels found themselves cast adrift in a maelstrom of uncertainty. They did not stand a chance, now stand defeated, humiliated, and captured by the army of Tree Creatures.

- **Give them to me, my friends, pled Hasdielle, addressing the trees, her voice echoing with eerie authority. I shall avenge your pain and suffering.**

The Trees swayed and creaked, their branches reaching out like gnarled hands, tightening the noose around Arakiba and Barrattiel. The very forest itself seemed to conspire against them, a living prison from which escape was all but possible. With a swift motion, Hasdielle seized the opportunity, sweeping the angels away from the clutches of the sentient woods. She ordered them to be carried to her hidden lair, a sinister chamber bathed in flickering candlelight.

Hasdielle, shrouded in an aura of malevolence, stood before her prisoners, Eto, Arakiba, and Barrattiel, a wicked grin twisting her lips. With a dark magic scroll clutched in her hand, she began to chant ancient incantations that resonated with the very essence of despair. The air crackled with an eerie energy as she invoked the powers that would open a portal to a sinister realm.

As her incantations reached their crescendo, the very fabric of reality tore open, revealing a portal to another world. From its depths emerged two colossal scorpions, their chitinous exoskeletons gleaming with a malefic sheen. Hasdielle's eyes gleamed with delight as she greeted the monstrous creatures with a twisted affection.

- **Welcome back to the living, my dear pets, purred Hasdielle, her voice dripping with perverse adoration.**

Hasdielle's command rang out through the air, ordering the first scorpion to approach Eto, the angelic prisoner, and siphon his ethereal essence. The creature obliged, its segmented body writhing as it unfurled a grotesque appendage resembling a serpent's head, complete with fanged teeth. With a ghastly hiss, the monstrous tail lunged toward Eto, seeking to sink its venomous fangs into his celestial form, draining his life force.

At that moment, Ethel stepped into the portal, the disorienting sensation only added to the chaos within her mind. Her heart raced, fuelled by the lingering echoes of her deepest fears that haunted her every thought. A sense of trepidation mingled with anticipation as she emerged on the other side, hoping to find solace or answers in this new realm.

But what she beheld shattered her hopes and plunged her into a pit of despair. Before her eyes, a malevolent act unfolded in all its abhorrent glory. Eto, her angelic partner, now stood before her, weakened and drained of their very essence. The sight struck Ethel like a physical blow, her heart sinking into the depths of sorrow.

A surge of horror coursed through her veins, mingling with a fierce sense of indignation. How could anyone unleash such dark and sickening magic upon another? The weight of her emotions threatened to consume her, yet Ethel could not bear the silence any longer. With trembling hands and a voice quivering with both fear and determination, Ethel spoke out against the unspeakable act. Her words carried the raw intensity of her emotions, echoing through the realm, challenging the very fabric of the twisted reality she found herself in.

She refused to accept the darkness that threatened to engulf them all. With each word, she fought against the oppressive shadows, offering a glimmer of hope amidst the bleakness. Her spirit aflame with a fiery resolve, Ethel raise the sword she kept from her last encounter. Hasdielle's attention was drawn to Ethel's presence, her eyes narrowing with a mixture of annoyance and curiosity. Sensing a disturbance in her plans, she swiftly issued a command to attack. The scorpions turned their attention toward Ethel, their pincers clacking with anticipation.

With a surge of determination, Ethel unleashed her own fury upon the oncoming scorpion. Her blade cleaved through the air with deadly precision, striking true as it severed the tail that had been draining the life from her knocked-out friend.

But that came at a heavy price, as the second scorpion struck back from the shadow. Its venomous stinger pierced through her armour, injecting a paralyzing toxin into her veins. Ethel's body went limp, collapsing to the ground, a prisoner in her own motionless form. Though her body was paralyzed, her mind remained acutely aware, trapped in a nightmarish existence. Ethel lay there, conscious but immobilized. The air reeked with the scent of despair, as the sorceress Hasdielle revealed her dark power. Ethel, paralyzed but conscientious, witnessed the horrors of the supernatural. She fought to retain her sanity within the confines of her paralyzed vessel.

- Ah, you are awakened, flirted Hasdielle. The time has come to feed, my dear. But fear not, I won't consume you entirely. Your essence, however, will be a delectable morsel.
- You... you're an angel, voiced Ethel with a mix of horror and disbelief. How can you be so monstrous to your own kind?
- Monstrous, perhaps, responded Hasdielle, but not in the way you think. I won't devour your flesh, my pet, but rather the very essence of your being. It shall be a feast beyond compare! You can judge me, but once you have a taste, you grow quickly addicted. If you are gentle, I can have you taste your friends before sucking the life out, drinking from your lips! I told you, I like you!

Hasdielle turned towards her pet Scorpion and caressed it on the head, only to brutally and swiftly plunge her sword inside his brain. Then, she severed his head shape tail and started drinking the essence extracted. The effect was spontaneous, filling the Dark Angel with pure angelic power. Just as Hasdielle believed their victory was secure, a sudden disturbance shattered the tranquillity. A strange creature emerged from the portal, a hooded half angel-like creature appeared and charged her head-on.

Hasdielle, caught off guard by the unexpected turn of events, recognized something eerily familiar in their opponent's fighting style. As the clash of blades intensified, the mysterious half-angel creature drove a knife deep into Hasdielle's form.

Hasdielle, poised to counterattack, hesitated for a brief moment. The realization of their own impending defeat flashed across their face. But before they could retaliate, the half-angel creature enveloped her within its wings, one angelic and the other burned beyond recognition, still smoking. Hasdielle was not one to be taken without a fight, from her newly consumed power, flames came out of her hands, which she applied to the side of the face she could recognize. Ethel witnessed the whole scene but could not intervene as she was still paralyzed. Only could she move her right arm.

As the 2 fought, Ethel saw the duo falling near her. She turned around and saw within reach, the snake-headed tail cut on the ground. She reached out and grabbed the slimy tail. As Hasdielle was burning the half-angel creature, she stepped closer to Ethel.

Ethel seized the opportunity to stab Hasdielle in her throat with the deadly tail, using it to cut through the delicate angelic skin of Hasdielle. That was a great blow, but not enough to stop the Dark Angel. Her future self, wounded but not dead yet, capitalized on the moment to engulf Hasdielle, enrolling her with her wings caught on fire and summoning her angelic power as they both were falling into the portal. As the celestial light appeared, both exploded like a bomb, bringing down the portal on them.

The portal collapsed behind them, severing the connection between the lair and the outside world. Ethel regained control of her body, quickly picked up her future sword from the ground and freed Eto. He was lifeless. She looked around and found the other snakehead's tail on the ground. She made Eto drink his own essence, whatever was left of it.

Ethel severed the ties of the sentinels and all rushed out of the cavern before the whole thing collapsed from the aftershock of the explosion.

This is 𝔚𝔥𝔦𝔰𝔭𝔢𝔯 𝔬𝔣 𝔇𝔞𝔯𝔨𝔫𝔢𝔰𝔰, the third volume of 𝔏𝔢𝔤𝔢𝔫𝔡𝔰 𝔬𝔣 𝔇𝔢𝔰𝔱𝔦𝔫𝔶.

Charon
GOD OF THE DEAD SEA

LEGENDS
OF
DESTINY

Epilogue

by Dr. BAK NGUYEN AND WILLIAM BAK

$\mathfrak{B}$ack in the hallowed halls of Heaven, Ethel stood before the Council, a solemn expression etched upon her face. Her voice quivered with a mix of trepidation and determination as she relayed the details of their mission, carefully omitting the encounter with her future self. The Council listened intently, their eyes bearing the weight of wisdom and judgment.

Ethel spoke of the battle with Hasdielle, recounting her valiant efforts to vanquish the fallen angel. However, skepticism hung in the air, and her words seemed to fall upon disbelieving ears. The council members exchanged glances, a silent understanding passing between them. It was as if they had already woven a different version of the story, one where the credit for Hasdielle's demise was bestowed upon Arakiba and Barrattiel, the revered sentinels.

Inwardly, Ethel seethed with a mix of frustration and disappointment. The weight of their disbelief pressed heavily upon her shoulders, robbing her of the honour and recognition she deserved. But her heart was burdened by a deeper concern, one that surpassed the desire for validation.

While her fellow angels celebrated their given victory, Ethel's thoughts lingered on the ominous future she had glimpsed. The spectre of darkness loomed over her, and she grappled with the knowledge that her own choices could shape or shatter her destiny. It was not the loss of recognition that troubled her, but the knowledge that a path filled with shadows awaited her if she did not find a way to change it.

In the midst of her turmoil, Ethel found company in the presence of Eto, her loyal and steadfast friend. Once weak and clumsy, Eto had transformed into a source of unwavering support, even with only half of his previous power.

As the council concluded their deliberations, Ethel's heart remained heavy, burdened by the weight of her unspoken truth. She accepted their decision, knowing that her own path would be one of resilience and defiance. She had a destiny to forge, one that transcended the limitations imposed upon her by others.

***

In the fiery depths of Hell, the future Ethel and Hasdielle engaged in a cataclysmic battle that shook the very foundations of the underworld. Their clash unleashed a torrent of dark energy, crackling with malevolence. The air was thick with the stench of sulfur and despair as their powers collided with devastating force.

The clash reached its crescendo as an explosion erupted, consuming the surroundings in an infernal blaze. The searing flames enveloped both Ethel and Hasdielle, searing their bodies and intertwining their essences in a twisted union. In the midst of the chaos, a transformation occurred, birthing an entirely new being that emerged from the ashes.

From the ashes arose Herate, the half-beautiful and cruel demon. The fusion of Ethel's charred form and Hasdielle's sinister essence gave birth to a creature of unparalleled malevolence. Herate stood tall, her once-angelic features distorted and marred by the torment of the underworld. Flames danced upon her flesh, casting an eerie glow that accentuated her newly acquired cruelty.

Herate's eyes, once filled with innocence and hope, now glimmered with Sinistre intensity. The melding of Ethel and Hasdielle had given birth to a being driven by a twisted desire for power and dominance. She relished in the pain and suffering she could inflict upon others, finding pleasure in the screams that echoed through the damned realm.

Herate's voice echoed with a chilling resonance, dripping with malice. Her malevolent laughter pierced the air, a chilling symphony that heralded the arrival of a fearsome force in the realm of Hell. The birth of this cruel demon marked a turning point in the underworld, as her reign of terror began to cast a dark shadow over the damned souls trapped within its fiery depths.

And so, with each step she took, Herate solidified her reign as the cruel demon, her name echoing through the infernal abyss. The underworld quaked beneath her merciless rule, its inhabitants forever changed by the emergence of this malevolent force. Now that Hell was conquered, Herate turned her attention to what was once, home.

This is **Whisper of Darkness**, the third volume of **Legends of Destiny**.

ANNEX
GLOSSARY OF Dr. BAK's LIBRARY

1

1SELF -080

REINVENT YOURSELF FROM ANY CRISIS
BY Dr. BAK NGUYEN

1SELF is about reinventing yourself to rise from any crisis. Written in the midst of the COVID war, now more than ever, we need hope and the know-how to bridge the future. More than just the journey of Dr. Bak, this time, Dr. Bak is sharing his journey with mentors and people who built part of the world as we know it. Interviewed in this book, CHRISTIAN TRUDEAU, former CEO and FOUNDER of BCE EMERGIS (BELL CANADA), he also digitalized the Montreal Stock Exchange. RON KLEIN, American Innovator, inventor of the magnetic stripe of the credit card, of MLS (Multi-listing services) and the man who digitalized WALL STREET bonds markets.ANDRE CHATELAIN, former first vice-president of the MOVEMENT DESJARDINS. Dr. JEAN DE SERRES, former CEO of HEMA QUEBEC. These men created billions in values and have changed our lives, even without us knowing. They all come together to share their experiences and knowledge to empower each and everyone to emerge stronger from this crisis, from any crisis.

A

AFTERMATH -063
BUSINESS AFTER THE GREAT PAUSE
BY Dr. BAK NGUYEN & Dr. ERIC LACOSTE

In AFTERMATH, Dr. Bak joins forces with Community leader and philanthrope Dr. Eric Lacoste. Two powerful minds and forces of nature in the reaction to the worst economic meltdown in modern times. We are all victims of the CORONA virus. Both just like humans have learnt to adapt to survive, so is our economy. Most business structures and management philosophies are inherited from the age of industrialization and beyond. COVID-19 has shot down the world economy for months. At the time of the AFTERMATH, the truth is many corporations and organizations will either have to upgrade to the INFORMATION AGE or disappear. More than the INFORMATION upgrade, the era of SOCIAL MEDIA and the MILLENNIALS are driving a revolution in the core philosophy of all organizations. Profit is not king anymore, support is. In this time and age where a teenager with a social account can compete with the million dollars PR firm, social implication is now the new cornerstone. Those who will adapt will prevail and prosper, while the resistance and old guards will soon be forgotten as fossils of a past era.

ALPHA DENTISTRY vol. 1 -104
DIGITAL ORTHODONTIC FAQ
BY Dr. BAK NGUYEN

In ALPHA DENTISTRY, DIGITAL ORTHODONTICS FAQ, Dr. Bak is looking to democratize the science of dentistry, starting with orthodontics. In a word, he is sharing everything a patient needs to know on the matter in FAQ form. In order to make the knowledge complete and universal, Dr. Bak has invited Alpha Dentists from all around the world to join in and answer the same question. With Alpha Dentists from America and Europe, ALPHA DENTISTRY is the first effort to create a universal knowledge in the field of dentistry, starting with orthodontics. ALPHA DENTISTRY, DIGITAL ORTHODONTICS FAQ is in response to the COVID crisis, the shortage of staff crisis, and the effort to unify dentistry to the Information Age, as discussed in RELEVANCY and COVIDCONOMICS, THE DENTAL INDUSTRY.

ALPHA DENTISTRY vol. 1 -109
DIGITAL ORTHODONTIC FAQ ASSEMBLED EDITION

CANADA GERMANY INDIA USA SPAIN
BY Dr. BAK NGUYEN, Dr. PAUL OUELLETTE, Dr. PAUL DOMINIQUE, Dr. MARIA KUNSTADTER, Dr. EDWARD J. ZUCKERBERG, Dr. MASHA KHAGHANI, Dr. SUJATA BASAWARAJ, Dr. ALVA AURORA, Dr. JUDITH BÄUMLER, and Dr. ASHISH GUPTA

In ALPHA DENTISTRY, DIGITAL ORTHODONTICS FAQ, Dr. Bak is democratizing the science of dentistry, starting with orthodontics. In a word, he is sharing everything a patient needs to know on the matter in FAQ form, simple words you'll understand.10 International Alpha Doctors, from USA, Spain, Germany, India, and Canada are joining forces to make the knowledge complete and universal. ALPHA DENTISTRY is the first effort to create a universal knowledge in the field of dentistry, this is the orthodontics volume. This is the most ambitious book project in the History of Dentistry. ALPHA DENTISTRY is in response to the COVID crisis, the shortage of staff crisis, and the effort to unify dentistry to the Information Age, as discussed in RELEVANCY and COVIDCONOMICS, THE DENTAL INDUSTRY.

ALPHA DENTISTRY vol. 1 -113
DIGITAL ORTHODONTIC FAQ INTERNATIONAL EDITION

ENGLISH FRENCH GERMAN HINDI SPANISH
BY Dr. BAK NGUYEN, Dr. PAUL OUELLETTE, Dr. PAUL DOMINIQUE, Dr. MARIA KUNSTADTER, Dr. EDWARD J. ZUCKERBERG, Dr. MASHA KHAGHANI, Dr. SUJATA BASAWARAJ, Dr. ALVA AURORA, Dr. JUDITH BÄUMLER, and Dr. ASHISH GUPTA

In ALPHA DENTISTRY, DIGITAL ORTHODONTICS FAQ, Dr. Bak is democratizing the science of dentistry, starting with orthodontics. In a word, he is sharing everything a patient needs to know on the matter in FAQ form, simple words you'll understand.10 International Alpha Doctors, from USA, Spain, Germany, India, and Canada are joining forces to make the knowledge complete and universal. ALPHA DENTISTRY is the first effort to create a universal knowledge in the field of dentistry, this is the orthodontics volume. This is the most ambitious book project in the History of Dentistry. ALPHA DENTISTRY is in response to the COVID crisis, the shortage of staff crisis, and the effort to unify dentistry to the Information Age, as discussed in RELEVANCY and COVIDCONOMICS, THE DENTAL INDUSTRY.

ALPHA DENTISTRY vol. 2 -127
IMPLANTOLOGY FAQ ASSEMBLED EDITION

ALBANIA BRAZIL CANADA INDIA MALAYSIA PORTUGAL SPAIN USA
BY Dr. BAK NGUYEN, Dr. ERIC LACOSTE , Dr. PRETINDER SINGH, Dr. SANDEEP SINGH, Dr. ERIC PULVER, Dr. ARASH HAKHAMIAN, Dr. MAHSA KHAGHANI, Dr. BENNETE FERNANDES, Dr. RAQUEL ZITA GOMES, Dr. SANDRA FABIANO and Dr. GURIEN DEMIRAQI

In ALPHA DENTISTRY, IMPLANTOLOGY FAQ, Dr. Bak is democratizing the science of dentistry, with the sub-specialty of IMPLANTOLOGY, which expertise is shared between Periodontists, Oral Surgeons and Dentists. In a word, he is sharing everything a patient needs to know on the matter in FAQ form, simple words you'll understand.11 International Alpha Doctors, from USA, India, Portugal, Spain, Brazil, Malaysia, Albania and Canada are joining forces to make the knowledge complete and universal. ALPHA DENTISTRY is the first effort to create a universal knowledge in the field of dentistry, this is the IMPLANTOLOGY volume. This is the most ambitious book project in the History of Dentistry. The whole book is covered in English and each author with a different native tongue is also covering their chapters in their native language. ALPHA DENTISTRY is in response to the COVID crisis, the shortage of staff crisis, and the effort to unify dentistry to the Information Age, as discussed in RELEVANCY and COVIDCONOMICS, THE DENTAL INDUSTRY.

ALPHA DENTISTRY vol. 2 -128
IMPLANTOLOGY FAQ INTERNATIONAL EDITION

ALBANIAN ENGLISH FRANÇAIS GERMAN HINDI ITALIAN KANNADA MALAY MANDARIN PORTUGUESE SPANISH
BY Dr. BAK NGUYEN, Dr. ERIC LACOSTE , Dr. PRETINDER SINGH, Dr. SANDEEP SINGH, Dr. ERIC PULVER, Dr. ARASH HAKHAMIAN, Dr. MAHSA KHAGHANI, Dr. BENNETE FERNANDES, Dr. RAQUEL ZITA GOMES, Dr. SANDRA FABIANO and Dr. GURIEN DEMIRAQI

In ALPHA DENTISTRY, IMPLANTOLOGY FAQ, Dr. Bak is democratizing the science of dentistry, with the sub-specialty of IMPLANTOLOGY, which expertise is shared between Periodontists, Oral Surgeons and Dentists. In a word, he is sharing everything a patient needs to know on the matter in FAQ form, simple words you'll understand.11 International Alpha Doctors, from USA, India, Portugal, Spain, Brazil, Malaysia, Albania and Canada are joining forces to make the knowledge complete and universal. ALPHA DENTISTRY is the first effort to create a universal knowledge in the field of dentistry, this is the IMPLANTOLOGY volume. This is the most ambitious book project in the History of Dentistry. The whole book is covered in English and each author with a different native tongue is also covering their chapters in their native language. ALPHA DENTISTRY is in response to the COVID crisis, the shortage of staff crisis, and the effort to unify dentistry to the Information Age, as discussed in RELEVANCY and COVIDCONOMICS, THE DENTAL INDUSTRY.

ALPHA DENTISTRY vol. 3 -131
PAEDIATRIC FAQ ASSEMBLED EDITION

CANADA EGYPT GERMANY ITALY PERU UNITED ARAB EMIRATES USA
BY Dr. BAK NGUYEN, Dr. PAUL DOMINIQUE, Dr. RICHARD SIMPSON, Dr. AURORA ALVA, Dr. NOUR AMMAR, Dr. AILIN CABRERA-MATTA, Dr. NIDHI TANEJA, Dr. PIERLUIGI PELAGALLI, Dr. PRRIYA PORWAL

In ALPHA DENTISTRY, PAEDIATRIC FAQ, Dr. Bak is democratizing the science of dentistry, this time, focusing on children. From all of dentistry, this is the kindest and most humane specialty of DENTISTRY. From the USA to Germany, Peru to Egypt and Canada, experts around the world are joining this collaborative effort welcome, reassure, and empower parents and kids on their quest to a healthy mouth. ALPHA DENTISTRY is the first effort to create a universal knowledge in the field of dentistry, this is the PAEDIATRIC volume. This is the most ambitious book project in the History of Dentistry. The whole book is covered in English and each author with a different native tongue is also covering their chapters in their native language. ALPHA DENTISTRY is in response to the COVID crisis, the shortage of staff crisis, and the effort to unify dentistry to the Information Age, as discussed in RELEVANCY and COVIDCONOMICS, THE DENTAL INDUSTRY.

ALPHA DENTISTRY vol. 3 -132
PAEDIATRIC FAQ INTERNATIONAL EDITION

ENGLISH ARABIC FRANÇAIS ITALIAN SPANISH

BY Dr. BAK NGUYEN, Dr. PAUL DOMINIQUE, Dr. RICHARD SIMPSON, Dr. AURORA ALVA, Dr. NOUR AMMAR, Dr. AILIN CABRERA-MATTA, Dr. NIDHI TANEJA, Dr. PIERLUIGI PELAGALLI, Dr. PRRIYA PORWAL

In ALPHA DENTISTRY, PAEDIATRIC FAQ, Dr. Bak is democratizing the science of dentistry, this time, focusing on children. From all of dentistry, this is the kindest and most humane specialty of DENTISTRY. From the USA to Germany, Peru to Egypt and Canada, experts around the world are joining this collaborative effort welcome, reassure, and empower parents and kids on their quest to a healthy mouth. ALPHA DENTISTRY is the first effort to create a universal knowledge in the field of dentistry, this is the PAEDIATRIC volume. This is the most ambitious book project in the History of Dentistry. The whole book is covered in English and each author with a different native tongue is also covering their chapters in their native language. ALPHA DENTISTRY is in response to the COVID crisis, the shortage of staff crisis, and the effort to unify dentistry to the Information Age, as discussed in RELEVANCY and COVIDCONOMICS, THE DENTAL INDUSTRY.

ALPHA DENTISTRY vol. 4 -136
PAEDIATRIC DENTISTRY FAQ ASSEMBLED EDITION

ALBANIA AUSTRALIA CANADA GERMANY INDIA IRAN MALAYSIA SPAIN USA

BY Dr. BAK NGUYEN, Dr. ERIC LACOSTE, Dr. MAZIAR SHAHZAD DOWLATSHAHI, Dr. BENNETE FERNANDES, Dr. MEENU BHASIN, Dr. HASTEE BHANUSHALI, Dr. ROBERT M. PICK, Dr. AMIN MOTAMEDI, Dr. TIHANA DIVNIC-RESNIK, Dr. ARNE VON STERNHEIM, Dr. FERNANDO ARPÓN MORENO and Dr. GURIEN DEMIRAQI

In ALPHA DENTISTRY, PERIODONTICS FAQ, Dr. Bak is democratizing the science of dentistry, with the sub-specialty of PERIODONTOLOGY, which expertise is shared between Periodontists, Oral Surgeons and Dentists. In a word, he is sharing everything a patient needs to know on the matter in FAQ form, simple words you'll understand.11 International Alpha Doctors, from the USA, India, Australia, Iran, Malaysia, Albania and Canada are joining forces to make the knowledge complete and universal. ALPHA DENTISTRY is the first effort to create a universal knowledge in the field of dentistry, this is the PERIODONTICS volume. This is the most ambitious book project in the History of Dentistry. The whole book is covered in English and each author with a different native tongue is also covering their chapters in their native language. ALPHA DENTISTRY is in response to the COVID crisis, the shortage of staff crisis, and the effort to unify dentistry to the Information Age, as discussed in RELEVANCY and COVIDCONOMICS, THE DENTAL INDUSTRY.

ALPHA DENTISTRY vol. 4 -137
PAEDIATRIC DENTISTRY FAQ INTERNATIONAL EDITION
 ENGLISH FRENCH GERMAN HINDI ITALIAN MANDARIN MALAY ARABIC
SPANISH SHQIP
BY Dr. BAK NGUYEN, Dr. ERIC LACOSTE, Dr. MAZIAR SHAHZAD DOWLATSHAHI, Dr. BENNETE FERNANDES, Dr. MEENU BHASIN, Dr. HASTEE BHANUSHALI, Dr. ROBERT M. PICK, Dr. AMIN MOTAMEDI, Dr. TIHANA DIVNIC-RESNIK, Dr. ARNE VON STERNHEIM, Dr. FERNANDO ARPÓN MORENO and Dr. GURIEN DEMIRAQI

In ALPHA DENTISTRY, PERIODONTICS FAQ, Dr. Bak is democratizing the science of dentistry, with the sub-specialty of PERIODONTOLOGY, which expertise is shared between Periodontists, Oral Surgeons and Dentists. In a word, he is sharing everything a patient needs to know on the matter in FAQ form, simple words you'll understand.11 International Alpha Doctors, from the USA, India, Germany, Spain, Australia, Iran, Malaysia, Albania and Canada are joining forces to make the knowledge complete and universal. ALPHA DENTISTRY is the first effort to create a universal knowledge in the field of dentistry, this is the PERIODONTICS volume. This is the most ambitious book project in the History of Dentistry. The whole book is covered in English and each author with a different native tongue is also covering their chapters in their native language. ALPHA DENTISTRY is in response to the COVID crisis, the shortage of staff crisis, and the effort to unify dentistry to the Information Age, as discussed in RELEVANCY and COVIDCONOMICS, THE DENTAL INDUSTRY.

ALPHA DENTISTRY vol. 5 -138
PAEDIATRIC DENTISTRY FAQ ASSEMBLED EDITION
 AUSTRALIA CANADA FRANCE LITHUANIA PERU TURKEY UKRAINE USA
BY Dr. BAK NGUYEN, Dr. JULIO REYNAFARJE, Dr. LINA DUSEVIČIŪTĖ, Dr. NAZARIY MYKHAYLYUK, Dr. CLAUDE MOUAFO, Dr. MANOJ RAJAN, Dr. LOUIS KAUFMAN, Dr. LILIAN SHI and Dr. YASEMIN OZKAN

In ALPHA DENTISTRY, COSMETIC DENTISTRY FAQ, Dr. Bak is democratizing the science of dentistry, with the sub-specialty of COSMETIC DENTISTRY, which expertise is shared between Prosthodontists and Dentists. In a word, he is sharing everything a patient needs to know on the matter in FAQ form, simple words you'll understand. International Alpha Doctors, from the USA, France, Peru, Lithuania, Ukraine, Australia, Turkey and Canada are joining forces to make the knowledge complete and universal.ALPHA DENTISTRY is the first effort to create a universal knowledge in the field of dentistry, this is the COSMETIC DENTISTRY volume. This is the most ambitious book project in the History of Dentistry. The whole book is covered in English and each author with a different native tongue is also covering their chapters in their native language. ALPHA DENTISTRY is in response to the COVID crisis, the shortage of staff crisis, and the effort to unify dentistry to the Information Age, as discussed in RELEVANCY and COVIDCONOMICS, THE DENTAL INDUSTRY.

ALPHA DENTISTRY vol. 5 -139
PAEDIATRIC DENTISTRY FAQ INTERNATIONAL EDITION
🏴 ENGLISH 🏴 ARABIC 🏴 FRENCH 🏴 🏴 LITHUANIAN 🏴 SPANISH 🏴 UKRAINIAN
BY Dr. BAK NGUYEN, Dr. JULIO REYNAFARJE, Dr. LINA DUSEVIČIŪTÉ, Dr. NAZARIY MYKHAYLYUK, Dr. CLAUDE MOUAFO, Dr. MANOJ RAJAN, Dr. LOUIS KAUFMAN, Dr. LILIAN SHI and Dr. YASEMIN OZKAN

In ALPHA DENTISTRY, COSMETIC DENTISTRY FAQ, Dr. Bak is democratizing the science of dentistry, with the sub-specialty of COSMETIC DENTISTRY, which expertise is shared between Prosthodontists and Dentists. In a word, he is sharing everything a patient needs to know on the matter in FAQ form, simple words you'll understand. International Alpha Doctors, from the USA, France, Peru, Lithuania, Ukraine, Australia, Turkey and Canada are joining forces to make the knowledge complete and universal.ALPHA DENTISTRY is the first effort to create a universal knowledge in the field of dentistry, this is the COSMETIC DENTISTRY volume. This is the most ambitious book project in the History of Dentistry. The whole book is covered in English and each author with a different native tongue is also covering their chapters in their native language. ALPHA DENTISTRY is in response to the COVID crisis, the shortage of staff crisis, and the effort to unify dentistry to the Information Age, as discussed in RELEVANCY and COVIDCONOMICS, THE DENTAL INDUSTRY.

ALPHA LADDERS -075
CAPTAIN OF YOUR DESTINY
BY Dr. BAK NGUYEN & JONAS DIOP

In ALPHA LADDERS, Dr. Bak is sharing his private conversation and board meetings with 2 of his trusted lieutenants, strategist Jonas Diop and international Counsellor, Brenda Garcia. As both Dr. Bak and ALPHA brands are gaining in popularity and traction, it was time to get the movement to the next level. Now, it's about building a community and helping everyone willing to become ALPHAS to find their powers. Dr. Bak is a natural recruiter of ALPHAS and peers. He also spent the last 20 years plus, training and mentoring proteges. Now comes the time to empower more and more proteges to become ALPHAS. ALPHAS LADDERS is the journey of how Dr. Bak went from a product of Conformity to rise into a force of Nature, known as a kind tornado. In ALPHA LADDERS Jonas pushed Dr. Bak to retrace each of the steps of his awakening, steps that we can break down and reproduce for ourselves. The goal is to empower each willing individual to become the ultimate Captain of his or her destiny, and to do it, again and again. Welcome to the Alphas.

ALPHA LADDERS 2 -081
SHAPING LEADERS AND ACHIEVERS
BY Dr. BAK NGUYEN & BRENDA GARCIA

In ALPHA LADDERS 2, Dr. Bak is sharing the second part of his private conversation and board meetings with his trusted lieutenants. This time it is with international Counsellor, Brenda Garcia that the dialogue is taking place. In this second tome, the journey is taken to the next level. If the first tome was about the WHYs and the HOWs at an individual level, this tome is about the WHYs and the HOWs at the societal level. Through the lens of her background in international relations and diplomacy, Brenda now has the mission to help Dr. Bak establish structures, not only for his emerging organization and legacy, THE ALPHAS, but to also inspire all the other leaders and structures of our society. To do this, Brenda is taking Dr. Bak on an anthropological, sociological and philosophical journey to revisit different historical key moments in various fields and eras, going as far back as ancient Greece at the dawn of democracy, all the way to the golden era of modern multilateralism embodied by the UN structure. Learning from the legacies of prominent figures going from Plato to Ban Ki-Moon, Martin Luther King or Nelson Mandela, to Machiavelli, Marx and Simone de Beauvoir, Brenda and Dr. Bak are attempting to grasp the essence of structure and hierarchy, their goal being to empower each willing individual to become the ultimate Captain of their success, to climb up the ladders no matter how high it is, and to build their legacy one step at a time.

ALPHA MASTERMIND vol. 1 -116
THE SUPERHERO'S SYNDROME
BY Dr. BAK NGUYEN

ALPHA MASTERMIND, THE SUPER HERO'S SYNDROME, is not a superhero book, but it is the tale of every leader, entrepreneur, and everyday hero facing their destiny and entourage. It uncovers how society sees our best elements and expects from them. It covers how family and friends feel and why they act as they do. But most importantly, it covers how Alphas can emerge unscathed from their growth to uncover their true powers and purpose. A veteran agent of change and difference maker, Dr. Bak is sharing his experience and secret of why and how surfing through family and society pressure without revolting and without kneeling. THE SUPERHERO'S SYNDROME is the first volume inspired by the MASTERMINDS sessions as Dr. Bak is mentoring Alpha apprentices. The superhero's syndrome came to the table as Alphas are struggling to fit in society, to keep their values and generosity while facing so much negativity all around. Welcome to the Alphas.

ALPHA MASTERMIND vol. 2 -117
SUPERCHARGING MOMENTUM
BY Dr. BAK NGUYEN

ALPHA MASTERMIND, SUPERCHARGING MOMENTUM, is what is discussed on the Alphas' Round Table. Entrepreneurs, Professional Athletes, Coaches, they are all rising from their passion and momentum. To start was the first ACT. It wasn't easy but they did. Now as a FOOTBALL star, what can be next, not to fall as a HAS BEEN? You wrote your first book, what is next? What comes next after 100 books?There are so many paths to finding your powers but there is only one that I know that will keep feeding them: MOMENTUM. If discovering your powers and purposes was a great journey, the sequel to that story is a much harder one to write, to walk, to thrive from. In every story, the hero needs to rise and to grow. How can one grow even more? SUPERCHARGING MOMENTUM is the 2nd volume inspired by the MASTERMINDS sessions as Dr. Bak is mentoring Alpha apprentices. Dr. Bak is not teaching, he is sharing what he faces and does to write his next life chapter, renewing and reinventing himself again and again. Welcome to the Alphas.

ALPHA MASTERMIND vol. 3 -118
RIDING DESTINY
BY Dr. BAK NGUYEN

In ALPHA MASTERMIND, RIDING DESTINY, Dr. Bak is taking you and his apprentices on the quest of rising. It will be for each to find their purpose and destiny, but the way leading there will be eased with Dr. Bak's guidance. To discover power was only the beginning, to yield power was a preparation journey, now it is about rendering power into a stream of ripple effect. "KNOW YOURSELF, KNOW THE OTHER, AND ONLY THEN, DEAL." - Dr. BAK. Well, the 2 first volumes were about knowing oneself, this one is about knowing the other and to start dealing. Once one finds power, it is barely the beginning of his or her quest. The process is not an easy one, going through separation, rejection, and denial. Then, there will be encounters of a new kind, those liberating instead of attaching.RIDING DESTINY, is the third volume inspired by the MASTERMINDS sessions as Dr. Bak is mentoring Alpha apprentices. This is about ROI on the energy invested and the one generated. Welcome to the Alphas.

AMONGST THE ALPHAS -058
BY Dr. BAK NGUYEN, with Dr. MARIA KUNSTADTER, Dr. PAUL OUELLETTE and Dr. JEREMY KRELL

In AMONGST THE ALPHAS, Dr. Bak opens the blueprint of the next level with the hope that everyone can be better, bigger, and wiser, but above all, a philosophy of Life that if, well applied, can bring inspiration to life. The Alphas rose in the midst of the COVID war as an International Collaboration to empower individuals to rise from the global crisis. Joining Dr. Bak are some of the world thinkers and achievers, the Alphas. Doctors, business people, thinkers, achievers, and influencers, are coming together to define what is an Alpha and his or her role, making the world a better place. This isn't the American dream, it is the human dream, one that can help you make History. Joining Dr. Bak are 3 Alpha authors, Dr. Maria Kunstadter, Dr. Paul Ouellette and Dr. Jeremy Krell. This book started with questions from coach Jonas Diop. Welcome to the Alphas.

AMONGST THE ALPHAS vol.2 -059
ON THE OTHER SIDE
BY Dr. BAK NGUYEN with Dr. JULIO REYNAFARJE, Dr. LINA DUSEVICIUTE and Dr. DUC-MINH LAM-DO

In AMONGST THE ALPHAS 2, Dr. Bak continues to explore the meaning of what it is to be an Alpha and how to act amongst Alphas, because as the saying taught us: alone one goes fast, together we go far. Some people see the problem. Some people look at the problem, some people created the problem. Some people leverage the problem into solutions and opportunities. Well, all of those people are Alphas. Networking and leveraging one another, their powers and reach are beyond measure. And one will keep the other in line too. Joining Dr. Bak are 3 Alphas from around the world coming together to share and collaborate, Dr. DUSEVICIUTE, Dr. LAM-DO and Dr. REYNAFARJE. This isn't the American dream, it is the human dream, one that can help you make History. Welcome to the Alphas.

AU PAYS DES PAPAS -106
BY Dr. BAK NGUYEN & WILLIAM BAK

On ne nait pas papa. On le devient. Dans sa quête d'être le meilleur papa possible pour William, Dr. Bak monte au pays des papas avec William à la recherche du papa parfait. Comme pour tout dans la vie, il doit exister une recette pour faire des papas parfaits. AU PAYS DES PAPAS est le récit des souvenirs des papas que Dr. Bak a croisé avant, alors et après qu'il soit devenu papa lui aussi. Une histoire drôle et innocente pour un Noël magique, ceci est la nouvelle aventure de William et de son papa, le Dr. Bak. Entre les livres de poulet, LEGENDS OF DESTINY et les des livres parentaux de Dr. Bak, AU PAYS DES PAPAS nous amène dans le monde magique de ces êtres magiques qui forgent des rêves, des vies et des destins.

AU PAYS DES PAPAS 2 -108
BY Dr. BAK NGUYEN & WILLIAM BAK

On ne nait pas papa, ça on le sait après le premier voyage AU PAYS DES PAPAS. Suite à leur première expédition, Dr. Bak et William ont compris qu'il n'y a pas de papas parfaits ni de recette pour faire des papas parfaits. Pourtant, les papas parfaits existent! Dans ce 2e récit AU PAYS DES PAPAS, William revient avec son papa, Dr. Bak, mais cette fois, c'est William qui dirige l'expédition.

Même s'il n'existe pas de recette pour faire des papas parfaits, il doit toutefois exister des façons de rendre son papa meilleur, version 2.0! C'est la nouvelle quête de William et du Dr. Bak, à la recherche de la mise-à-jour parfaite pour le meilleur papa 2.0 possible! William est déterminé à tout pour trouver la recette cette fois-ci! AU PAYS DES PAPAS 2 est le nouveau récit des aventures père-fils du Dr. Bak et de William Bak, après AU PAYS DES PAPAS 1, les livres de poulets, LEGENDS OF DESTINY et les BOOKS OF LEGENDS.

B

BOOTCAMP -071
BOOKS TO REWRITE MINDSETS INTO WINNING STATES OF MIND
BY Dr. BAK NGUYEN

In BOOTCAMP 8 BOOKS TO REWRITE MINDSETS INTO WINNING STATES OF MIND, Dr. Bak is taking you into his past, before the visionary entrepreneur, before the world records, before the Industry's disruptor status. Here are 8 of the books that changed Dr. Bak's thinking and, therefore, reset his evolution into the course we now know him for. BOOTCAMP: 8 BOOKS TO REWRITE MINDSETS INTO WINNING STATES OF MIND, is a Bootcamp of 8 weeks for anyone looking to experience Dr. Bak's training to become THE Dr. BAK you came to know and love. This book will summarize how each title changed Dr. Bak's mindset into a state of mind and how he applied that to rewrite his destiny. 8 books to read, that's 8 weeks of Bootcamp to access the power of your MIND and your WILL. Are you ready for a change?

BRANDING -044
BALANCING STRATEGY AND EMOTIONS
BY Dr. BAK NGUYEN

BRANDING is communication to its most powerful state. Branding is not just about communicating anymore but about making a promise, about establishing a relationship, and about generating an emotion. More than once, Dr. Bak proved himself to be a master, communicating and branding his ideas into flags attracting interest and influence, nationally and internationally. In BRANDING, Dr. Bak shares a very unique and personal journey, branding Dr. Bak. How does he go from Dr. Nguyen, a loved and respected dentist to becoming Dr. Bak, a world anchor hosting THE ALPHAS in the medical and financial world? More than a personal journey, BRANDING helps to break down the steps to elevate someone with nothing else but the force of his or her spirit. Welcome to the Alphas.

C

CHANGING THE WORLD FROM A DENTAL CHAIR -007
BY Dr. BAK NGUYEN

Since he has received the EY's nomination for entrepreneur of the year for his startup Mdex & Co, Dr. Bak Nguyen has pushed the opportunity to the next level. Speaker, author, and businessman, Dr. Bak is a true entrepreneur and industries' disruptor. To compensate for the startup's status of Mdex & Co, he challenged himself to write a book based on the EY's questionnaire to share an in-depth vision of his company. With "Changing the World from a dental chair" Dr. Bak is sharing his thought process and philosophy to his approach to the industry. Not looking to revolutionize but rather to empower, he became, despite himself, an industries disruptor: an entrepreneur who has established a new benchmark. Dr. Bak Nguyen is a cosmetic dentist and visionary businessman who won the GRAND HOMAGE prize of "LYS de la Diversité" 2016, for his contribution as a citizen and entrepreneur in the community. He also holds recognitions from the Canadian Parliament and the Canadian Senate. In 2003, he founded Mdex, a dental company upon which in 2018, he launched the most ambitious private endeavour to reform the dental industry, Canada-wide. He wrote seven books covering ENTREPRENEURSHIP, LEADERSHIP, QUEST of IDENTITY, and now, PROFESSION HEALTH. Philosopher, he has close to his heart the quest of happiness of the people surrounding him, patients, and colleagues alike. Those projects have allowed Dr. Nguyen to attract interest from the international and diplomatic community and he is now the centre of a global discussion on the wellbeing and the future of the health profession. It is in that matter that he shares with you his thoughts and encourages the health community to share their own stories.

CHAMPION MINDSET -039
LEARNING TO WIN
BY Dr. BAK NGUYEN & CHRISTOPHE MULUMBA

CHAMPION MINDSET is the encounter of the business world and the professional sports world. Industries' Disruptor Dr. BAK NGUYEN shares his wisdom and views with the HAMMER, CFL Football Star, Edmonton's Eskimos CHRISTOPHE MULUMBA on how to leverage the champion mindset to create successful entrepreneurs. Writing and challenging each other, they discovered the parallels and the difference of both worlds, but mainly, the recipe for leveraging from one to succeed in the other, from champions and entrepreneurs to WINNERS. Build and score your millions, it is a matter of mindset! This is CHAMPION MINDSET.

COMMENT ÉCRIRE UN LIVRE EN 30 JOURS -102
PAR Dr. BAK NGUYEN

Dans COMMENT ÉCRIRE UN LIVRE EN 30 JOURS, après plus de 100 livres écrits en 4 ans, le Dr Bak revisite son premier succès, le livre dans lequel il a partagé son art et sa structure d'écriture de livres. Encore et encore, le Dr Bak a prouvé que non seulement le contenu est important, mais ce sont la structure et le processus qui rendent les livres. L'inspiration n'est que le début. Si vous envisagez d'écrire votre premier livre, ceci est votre chance. Si vous y pensez, faites-le, et aussi vite que possible. Écrire votre premier livre vous libérera de votre passé et vous ouvrira les portes de votre avenir! Tout le monde a une histoire qui mérite d'être partagée! Par où commencer, comment passer le MUR DE L'INSPIRATION, quelles sont les techniques pour apporter de la profondeur à votre histoire, comment structurer votre chapitre, combien de chapitres, comment avoir un livre, en un mois? Voilà les réponses que vous trouverez dans COMMENT ÉCRIRE UN LIVRE EN 30 JOURS. Vous trouverez un trésor de sagesse, un mentor et surtout, une confiance renouvelée pour écrire, que ce soit, votre premier, deuxième ou même 10e livre. Au fait, le Dr. Bak a écrit ce livre et l'a fait publier en 6 jours. Bienvenu(e)s aux Alphas.

COMMENT ÉCRIRE 2 LIVRES EN 10 JOURS -115
Par WILLIAM & Dr. BAK NGUYEN

Dans COMMENT ÉCRIRE 2 LIVRES EN 10 JOURS, William Bak s'attaque au succès de son père, COMMENT ÉCRIRE UN LIVRE EN 30 JOURS. Cette fois-ci, père et fils font équipe pour vous partager l'art d'écrire de la fiction. Comme le titre le mentionne, William doit écrire ce livre et le suivant en 10 jours. Pour ne pas vous induire en erreur, écrire votre premier livre de fiction prendra plus que 10 jours. Cependant, les procédés contenus dans ce livre vous aideront à accélérer votre production et à porter votre créativité à des niveaux inégalés. William a 12 ans et déjà, il a signé 36 livres dont la plupart sont de la fiction. En ce sens, il est un vétéran auteur, un qui a connu les hauts et les bas du manque d'inspiration. Au côté de William, Dr. Bak se prête aussi au jeux de démolir son propre succès et le remplacer par une nouvelle marque. Père et fils, ils vous partagent leurs secrets et expérience à écrire un duo-choque depuis les derniers 4 ans. COMMENT ÉCRIRE 2 LIVRES EN 10 JOURS a commencé par une farce qui est rapidement devenu leur plus grand défi à ce jour, d'écrire 2 livres en 10 jours. Bienvenu(e)s aux Alphas.

COVIDCONOMIE -111
CONTRER L'INFLATION SANS TOUCHER LES TAUX D'INTÉRÊT
PAR Dr. BAK NGUYEN, ANDRÉ CHÂTEALAIN, TRANIE VO, FRANÇOIS DUFOUR, WILLIAM BAK

COVIDCONOMIE est l'ensemble des observations, analyses des phénomènes démographiques et économiques secondaires à la pandémie de la COVID-19. CONTRER L'INFLATION SANS TOUCHER LES TAUX D'INTÉRÊT, est la réflexion et plan macro des ALPHAS pour le CANADA et les ÉTATS-UNIS D'AMÉRIQUE dans un premier temps et un modèle économique pour l'ensemble des pays d'Occident.Joint par des leaders en finance et en économie, dont André Châtelain, ancien premier vice-président du MOUVEMENT DESJARDINS, le Dr. Bak met la table à des discussions inclusives et constructives pouvant changer le cours de l'Histoire dans l'intérêt des citoyens au quotidien.CONTRER L'INFLATION SANS TOUCHER LES TAUX D'INTÉRÊT, est un mémoire collectif des ALPHAS pour lutter contre l'inflation post-pandémique et éviter une récession internationale globale.

COVIDCONOMICS -112
TAMING INFLATION WITHOUT INCREASING INTEREST RATES
BY Dr. BAK NGUYEN, ANDRÉ CHÂTEALAIN, TRANIE VO, FRANÇOIS DUFOUR, WILLIAM BAK

COVIDCONOMICS, are the reflections, analysis and discussion of the ALPHAS, hosted by Dr. Bak to understand the demographic et economical trends post-COVID-19. TAMING INFLATION WITHOUT INCREASING INTEREST RATES is a macro plan by the ALPHAS for Canada and the USA which can inspire a new economical model for all of the Western worlds. Joined by leaders in finance as André Châtelain, former 1st Vice-President of the MOUVEMENT DESJARDINS, Dr. Bak is hosting an inclusive discussion to save our economy in these very troubled times as the country is still looking to get back on its feet from the Pandemic while wars are raging on multiple fronts. TAMING INFLATION WITHOUT INCREASING INTEREST RATES is our proposal to save the economy and our recovery from a global recession.

E

EMPOWERMENT -069

BY Dr. BAK NGUYEN

In EMPOWERMENT, Dr. Bak's 69th book, writing a book every 8 days for 8 weeks in a row to write the next world record of writing 72 books/36 months, Dr. Bak is taking a rest, sharing his inner feelings, inspiration, and motivation. Much more than his dairy, EMPOWERMENT is the key to walking in his footsteps and comprehending the process of an overachiever. Dr. Bak's helped and inspired countless people to find their voice, to live their dream, and to be the better version of themselves. Why is he sharing as much and keep sharing? Why is he going that fast, always further and further, why and how is he keeping his inspiration and momentum? Those are all the answers EMPOWERMENT will deliver to you. This book might be one of the fastest Dr. Bak has written, not because of time constraints but from inspiration, pure inspiration to share and to grow. There is always a dark side to each power, two faces to a coin. Well, this is the less prominent facet of Dr. Bak's Momentum and success, the road to his MINDSET.

F

FORCES OF NATURE -015
FORGING THE CHARACTER OF WINNERS
BY Dr. BAK NGUYEN

In FORCES OF NATURE, Dr. Bak is giving his all. This is his 15 books written within 15 months. It is the end of a marathon to set the next world record. For the occasion, he wanted to end with a big bang! How about a book with all of his biggest challenges? In a Quest of Identity, a journey looking for his name and powers, Dr. Bak is borrowing myths and legends to make this journey universal. Yes, this is Dr. Bak's mythology. Demons, heroes and Gods, there are forces of Nature that we all meet on our way for our name. Some will scare us, some will fight us, and some will manipulate us. We can flee, we can hide, we can fight. What we do will define our next encounter and the one after. A tale of personal growth, a journey to find power and purpose, Dr. Bak is showing us the path to freedom, the Path of Life. Welcome to the Alphas.

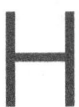

H

HORIZON, BUILDING UP THE VISION -045
VOLUME ONE
BY Dr. BAK NGUYEN

Dr. Bak is opening up to your demand! Many of you are following Dr. Bak online and are asking to know more about his lifestyle. This is how he has chosen to respond: sharing his lifestyle as he travelled the world and what he learnt in each city to come to build his Mindset as a driver and a winner. Here are 10 destinations (over 69 that will be followed in the next volumes...) in which he shares his journey. New York, Quebec, Paris, Punta Cana, Monaco, Los Angeles, Nice, and Holguin, the journey happened over twenty years.

HORIZON, ON THE FOOTSTEP OF TITANS -048
VOLUME TWO
BY Dr. BAK NGUYEN

Dr. Bak is opening up to your demand! Many of you are following Dr. Bak online and are asking to know more about his lifestyle. This is how he has chosen to respond: sharing his lifestyle as he travelled the world and what he learnt in each city to come to build his Mindset as a driver and a winner. Here are 9 destinations (over 72 that will follow in the next volumes...) in which he shares his journey. Hong Kong, London, Rome, San Francisco, Anaheim, and more..., the journey happened over twenty years. Dr. Bak is sharing with you his feelings, impressions, and how they shaped his state of mind and character into Dr. Bak. From a dreamer to a driver and a builder, the journey started when he was 3. Wealth is a state of mind, and a state of mind is the basis of the drive. Find out about the mind of an Industry's disruptor.

HORIZON, DREAMING OF THE FUTURE -068
VOLUME THREE
BY Dr. BAK NGUYEN

Dr. Bak is back. From the midst of confinement, he remembers and writes about what life was, when travelling was a natural part of Life. It will come back. Now more than ever, we need to open both our hearts and minds to fight fear and intolerance. Writing from a time of crisis, he is sharing the magic and psychological effect of seeing the world and how it has shaped his mindset. Here are 9 other destinations (over 75) in which he shares his journey. Beijing, Key West, Madrid, Amsterdam, Marrakech and more…, the journey happened over twenty years.

HOW TO TO BOOST YOUR CREATIVITY TO NEW HEIGHTS -088
BY Dr. BAK NGUYEN

In HOW TO BOOST YOUR CREATIVITY TO NEW HEIGHTS, Dr. Bak is sharing his secrets of creativity and insane production pace with the world. Up to lately, Dr. Bak shared his secrets about speed and momentum but never has he opened up about where he gets his inspiration, time and time again. To celebrate his new world record of writing 100 books in 4 years, Dr. Bak is joined by his proteges strategist Jonas Diop, international counsellor Brenda Garcia and prodigy William Bak for the writing of his secrets on creativity. Brenda, Jonas and William all have witnessed Dr. Bak's creativity. This time, they will stand in to ask the right questions to unleash that creative power in ways for others to follow the trail. Part of the MILLION DOLLAR MINDSET series, HOW TO BOOST YOUR CREATIVITY TO NEW HEIGHTS is Dr. Bak's open book to one of his superpowers.

HOW TO NOT FAIL AS A DENTIST -047
BY Dr. BAK NGUYEN

In HOW TO NOT FAIL AS A DENTIST, Dr. Bak is given 20 plus years of experience and knowledge of what it is to be a dentist on the ground. PROFESSIONAL INTELLIGENCE, FINANCIAL INTELLIGENCE and MANAGEMENT INTELLIGENCE are the fields that any dentist will have to master for a chance to succeed and a shot at happiness, practicing dentistry. Where ever you are starting your career as a new graduate or a veteran in the field looking to reach the next level, this is book smart and street smart all into one. This is Million Dollar Mindset applied to dentistry. We won't be making a millionaire out of you from this book, we will be giving you a shot at happiness and success. The million will follow soon enough.

HOW TO WRITE A BOOK IN 30 DAYS -042
BY Dr. BAK NGUYEN

In HOW TO WRITE A BOOK IN 30 DAYS, after more than 100 books written in 4 years, Dr. Bak is revisiting his first hit, the book in which he shared his craft and structure of how to write books. After 100 books, Dr. Bak proved that not only content is important, but what will keep the words coming are the structure and the process. If you are looking into writing your first book, this is your chance. If you are thinking about it, do it, and as fast as possible. Writing your first book will set you free from your past and open the doors to your own future! Everyone has a story worth telling! Where to start, how to get by the INSPIRATIONAL WALL, what are the techniques to bring depth into your storytelling, how to structure your chapter, how many chapters, how to have a book, in a month? These are the answers you will find within HOW TO WRITE A BOOK IN 30 DAYS. You will find a wealth of wisdom from his experience writing your first, second or even 10th book. Dr. Bak is sharing his secrets writing books. By the way, he wrote this book and got it published within 6 days. Welcome to the Alphas.

HOW 2 WRITE 2 BOOKS IN 10 DAYS -114
BY WILLIAM & Dr. BAK NGUYEN

HOW 2 WRITE 2 BOOKS IN 10 DAYS, is William Bak takes on his father's hit, HOW TO WRITE A BOOK IN 30 DAYS. This time, William is covering the art of writing fiction. As mentioned in the title, William is writing this book and the next one within 10 days. Just not to mislead you, writing fiction will take longer, but once you have done all your prep work and research, it can be written as quickly. William is only 12 and already, he has signed 35 books. Most of his books are fiction, so on the matter, he is a veteran author, one with much experience of the ups and downs when it comes to writing books and getting them to the finish line Joining him is Dr. Bak who is sharing his secrets of writing fiction too. What does it take, how different it is from writing non-fictional books and what does it take to inspire and motivate his 12-year-old son to write as much, matching his world record pace? HOW 2 WRITE 2 BOOKS IN 10 DAYS is a joke between 2 world record authors teasing one another as they keep raising the bar higher and higher. Welcome to the Alphas.

HOW TO WRITE A SUCCESSFUL BUSINESS PLAN -049
BY Dr. BAK NGUYEN & ROUBA SAKR

In HOW TO WRITE A SUCCESSFUL BUSINESS PLAN, Dr. Bak is given 20 plus years of experience and knowledge of what it is to be an entrepreneur and more importantly, how to have the investors and banks on your side. Being an entrepreneur is surely not something you learn from school, but there are steps to master so you can communicate your views and vision. That's the only way you will have financing. Writing a business is only not a mandatory stop only for the bankers, but an essential step for every entrepreneur, to know the direction and what's coming next. A business plan is also not set in stone, if there is a truth in business is that nothing will go as planned. Writing down your business plan the first time will prepare you to adapt and overcome the challenges and surprises. For most entrepreneurs, a business is a passion. To most investors and all banks, a business is a system. Your business plan is the map to that system. However unique your ideas and business are, the mapping follows the same steps and pattern.

HOW TO SEDUCE ANYONE -129
BY Dr. BAK NGUYEN

In HOW TO SEDUCE ANYONE, Dr. Bak is pushed by 2 of his female apprentices to share the secret behind his smile and influence. Seduction has many facets and can be leveraged in so many ways. Dr. Bak's way is to seduce without seducing, with tricks or fireworks. He, himself never saw himself as a seducer, until asked to share his skills and knowledge on the matter. Everything in life is about connecting and interacting with others. So it is safe to say that all of our social life is about seducing, even when sharing. To learn to eat, to talk, to wrap, and to open is an old Vietnamese saying about the ways of life. Well, to Dr. Bak, it is much simpler than that. Seduction is about being confident enough to be available to the other person, available to listen and to empower. It is all about what the other person feels in your presence which is the key to your influence and charm. Easier said than done! Well in this journey, you are following Dr. Bak along with Alpha Coach Mel and Alpha host Natasha DG to uncover the ways to seduce without seducing, to gain the minds and hearts of those you touch without compromising or overselling yourself. HOW TO SEDUCE ANYONE is a conversation with Dr. Bak, straight from the heart and without filtre. Based on a podcast interview from WOMAN UP and more than 3 decades of winning the hearts of those he touches, these are Dr. Bak's secrets. Welcome to the Alphas.

HUMILITY FOR SUCCESS -051
BALANCING STRATEGY AND EMOTIONS
BY Dr. BAK NGUYEN

HUMILITY FOR SUCCESS is exploring the emotional discomforts and challenges champions, and overachievers put themselves through. Success is never done overnight and on the way, just like the pain and the struggles aren't enough, we are dealing with the doubts, the haters, and those who like to tell us how to live our lives and what to do. At the same time, nothing of worth can be achieved alone. Every legend has a cast of characters, allies, mentors, companions, rivals, and foes. So one needs the key to social behaviour. HUMILITY FOR SUCCESS is exploring the matter and will help you sort out beliefs from values, and peers from friends. Humility is much more about how we see ourselves than how others see us. For any entrepreneur and champion, our daily is to set our mindset right, and to perfect our skills, not to fit in. There is a world where CONFIDENCE grows in synergy with HUMILITY. As you set the right label on the right belief, you will be able to grow and leave the lies and haters far behind. This is HUMILITY FOR SUCCESS.

HYBRID 011
THE MODERN QUEST OF IDENTITY
BY Dr. BAK NGUYEN

I

IDENTITY 004
THE ANTHOLOGY OF QUESTS
BY Dr. BAK NGUYEN

What if John Lennon was still alive and running for president today? What kind of campaign will he be running? IDENTIFY -THE ANTHOLOGY OF QUESTS is about the quest each of us has to undertake, sooner or later, THE QUEST OF IDENTITY. Citizens of the world, aim to be one, the one, one whole, one unity, made of many. That's the anthology of life! Start with your one, find your unity, and your legend will start. We are all small-minded people anyway! We need each other to be one! We need each other to be happy, so we, so you, so I, can be happy. This is the chorus of life. This is our song! Citizens of the world, I salute you! This is the first tome of the IDENTITY QUEST. FORCES OF NATURE (tome 2) will be following in SUMMER 2021. Also under development, Tome 3 - THE CONQUEROR WITHIN will start production soon.

INDUSTRIES DISRUPTORS 006
BY Dr. BAK NGUYEN

INDUSTRIES DISRUPTORS is a strange title, one that sparkles mixed feelings. A disruptor is someone making a difference, and since we, in general, do not like change, the label is mostly negative. But a disruptor is mostly someone who sees the same problem and challenge from another angle. The disruptor will tackle that angle and come up with something new from something existent. That's evolution! In INDUSTRIES DISRUPTORS, Dr. Bak is joining forces with James Stephan-Usypchuk to share with us what is going on in the minds and shoes of those entrepreneurs disrupting the old habits. Dr. Bak is changing the world from a dental chair, disrupting the dental, and now the book industry. James is a maverick in the Intelligence space, from marketing to Artificial Intelligence. Coming from very different backgrounds and industries, they end up telling very similar stories. If disruptors change the world, well, their story proves that disruptors can be made and forged. Here's the recipe. Here are their stories.

KRYPTO 040
TO SAVE THE WORLD
BY Dr. BAK NGUYEN & ILYAS BAKOUCH

L

L'ART DE TRANSFORMER DE LA SOUPE EN MAGIE -103

PAR Dr. BAK NGUYEN

Dans L'ART DE TRANSFORMER DE LA SOUPE EN MAGIE, Dr. Bak remonte aux sources pour connaître la source de son génie et la recette qui a été transféré à son fils, William Bak, auteur et record mondial dès l'âge de 8 ans. Docteur en médecine dentaire, entrepreneur, écrivain record mondial, musicien, Dr. Bak est d'abord et avant tout un fils qui a une maman qui croit en lui. L'ART DE TRANSFORMER DE LA SOUPE EN MAGIE est dédié à la recette du génie, celle qui pousse une mère a mijoté les ingrédients de l'espoir dans un bouillon d'amour, à y ajuster un zeste de bonheur et un brin d'ambition. Dans la lignée des livres parentaux de Dr. Bak, L'ART DE TRANSFORMER DE LA SOUPE EN MAGIE est dédié à la première femme dans sa vie, celle qui a tracé son destin et celle qui l'a cultivée.

LEADERSHIP -003
PANDORA'S BOX

BY Dr. BAK NGUYEN

LEADERSHIP, PANDORA'S BOX is 21 presidential speeches for a better tomorrow for all of us. It aims to drive HOPE and motivation into each and every one of us. Together we can make the difference, we hold such power. Covering themes from LOYALTY to GENEROSITY, from FREEDOM and INTELLIGENCE to DOUBTS and DEATH, this is not the typical presidential or motivational speeches that we are used to. LEADERSHIP PANDORA'S BOX will surf your emotions first, only to dive with you to touch the core and soul of our meaning: to matter. This is not a Quest of Identity, but the cry to rally as a species, raise our heads toward the future and move forward as a WHOLE. Not a typical Dr. Bak's book, LEADERSHIP, PANDORA'S BOX is a must-read for all of you looking for hope and purpose, all of us, citizens of the world.

LEADERSHIP vol. 1 (ALPHA DENTISTRY) -121
CHANGING THE WORLD FROM A DENTAL CHAIR

ALBANIA BRAZIL CANADA HUNGARY MALAYSIA SPAIN USA

BY Dr. BAK NGUYEN, Dr. MAHSA KHAGHANI, Dr. NAGY KATALIN, with guest authors Dr. PAUL DOMINIQUE, Dr. PAUL OUELLETTE, Dr. GURIEN DEMIRAQI, Dr. BENNETE FERNANDES, Dr. SANDRA FABIANO, Dr. ARASH HAKHAMIAN and Dr. MARILYN SANDOR

ALPHA DENTISTRY proudly presents LEADERSHIP, CHANGING THE WORLD FROM A DENTAL CHAIR. This time, Dr. Bak is leading the charge of rebuilding the foundations of the dental industry, especially after the light shed by COVID. More than once, populations from all around the world have expressed their negative perceptions and uneasy feelings about the dental industry. For decades, we turned deaf and blinded to these criticisms. In the worse health crisis of our lifetime, our specialists, experts and all our doctors were benched, despite being health professionals... The message is clear, the whole field must be rethought and better adapted to our modern societies. In the hope of bringing new ideas and philosophies, Dr. Bak is joined by Dr. Mahsa Khaghani from Spain and Dr. Nagy Katalin from Hungary, along with Dr. Paul Dominique, Dr. Paul Ouellette, Dr. Arash Hakhamian and Dr. Marilyn Sandor from the USA, Dr. Gurien Demiraqi from Albania, Dr. Bennete Fernandes from Malaysia, and Dr. Sandra Fabiano from Brazil to lead this history journey looking to modernize and make dentistry more accessible and affordable. It will take leadership and courage to assemble all of the world's dental industry and bridge the gaps to a better future. It starts by listening and then, dialoguing. LEADERSHIP is an inclusive dialogue. This is the first volume of this new series in which International Dental leaders will be joining forces to rebuild Dentistry. First mission: lower the costs of dentistry. Welcome to the Alphas.

LEGENDS OF DESTINY vol.1 -101
THE PROLOGUES OF DESTINY
BY Dr. BAK NGUYEN & WILLIAM BAK

The war between the forces of death and the legions of life lasted for centuries, ravaging most of the twin planets, Destiny and Earth. The end was so imminent that even the Gods got involved to save Life from eternal doom. Heroes rise and fall from all sides. Some fight for good, others, for evil. Gods, titans, angels, and demons all took sides in the war. Gods fight and kill other gods. Angel fights alongside demons, striking down Gods and Titans, and rival angels. The war lasted for so long that no one even remembers what they were fighting for. Some fight for domination while others, just to survive. The war ravages Destiny, the twin sister of planet Earth to the brink of annihilation. All eyes now turn to Earth. As the balance of the creation itself hands in the balance, a species emerges as holding the balance to victory: mankind. For the future of Humanity, of Gods and men and everything in between, this is the last stand of Destiny, a last chance for life.

LEGENDS OF DESTINY vol.2 -107
THE BOOK OF ELVES
BY Dr. BAK NGUYEN & WILLIAM BAK

Caught between the Orcs invading from the center of Destiny, the Angels raining down and the Demons eating from within, the Elves are turning from their old beliefs and Gods for salvation. For Millennials, Elves turned to Odin and the Forces of Nature for answers and guidance. Since the imminent destruction of their kingdoms and cities, a new God is offering Hope, Kal, the old God of fire. Kal gave them more than Hope, he gave the elves who turned to him for passage to a new world. But more than hope, more than fear, Elves value honour and Destiny. At least their old guards and heroes do. With their world crumbling down, and the rise of the new and younger generations, Elf's society seems to be at the crossroad of evolution. It is convert or die. Or die fighting or die kneeling. The Book of Elves is the story of a civilization facing its fate in the blink of destruction.

LE POUVOIR DE LA SÉDUCTION -130
PAR Dr. BAK NGUYEN

Dans LE POUVOIR DE LA SÉDUCTION, le Dr Bak est poussé par deux de ses protégées Alphas à partager le secret derrière son sourire et son influence. La séduction a de nombreuses facettes et peut être utilisée à de nombreuses fins. Séduire sans séduire, est la philosophie du Dr. Bak, sans astuces ni feux d'artifice. Lui-même ne s'est jamais considéré comme un séducteur jusqu'à ce qu'on le sollicite pour ses compétences et secrets en la matière. La vie sociale est une grande séduction. Que ce soit d'interagir, partager, soigner, enseigner, même aider, tout revient sur l'aptitude de chacun à mettre en confiance. Apprendre à manger, à parler, à emballer et à ouvrir est un vieux dicton vietnamien sur la façon de vivre. Eh bien, pour le Dr Bak, c'est beaucoup plus simple que cela. La séduction consiste à être suffisamment confiant pour pouvoir s'oublier et être disponible pour l'autre. La clé de la séduction et de l'influence est dans comment les autres se sentent en notre présence. LE POUVOIR DE LA SÉDUCTION est une conversation entre avec la coach Mel et l'animatrice Natasha DG, le Dr Bak et vous. Ce livre est inspiré du podcast WOMAN UP et sur plus de 3 décennies à conquérir les cœurs et le respect de ceux qu'il touche. Voici les secrets du Dr Bak. Bienvenu(e) aux Alphas.

LEVERAGE -014
COMMUNICATION INTO SUCCESS
BY Dr. BAK NGUYEN

In LEVERAGE COMMUNICATION TO SUCCESS, Dr. Bak shares his secret and mindsets to elevate an idea into a vision and a vision into an endeavour. Some endeavours will be a project, some others will become companies, and some will grow into a movement. It does not matter, each started with great communication. Communication is a very vast concept, education, sale, sharing, empowering, coaching, preaching, and entertaining. Those are all different kinds of communication. The intent differs, the audiences vary, and the messages are unique but the frame can be templated and mastered. In LEVERAGE COMMUNICATION TO SUCCESS, Dr. Bak is loyal to his core, sharing only what he knows best, what he has done himself. This book is dedicated to communicating successfully in business.

MASTERMIND, 7 WAYS INTO THE BIG LEAGUE -052
BY Dr. BAK NGUYEN & JONAS DIOP

MASTERMIND, 7 WAYS INTO THE BIG LEAGUE is the result of the encounter between business coach Jonas Diop and Dr. Bak. As a professional podcaster and someone always seeking the truth and ways to leverage success and performance, coach Jonas is putting Dr. Bak to the test, one that should reveal his secret to overachieve month after month, accumulating a new world record every month. Follow those two great minds as they push each other to surpass themselves, each in their own way and own style. MASTERMIND, 7 WAYS INTO THE BIG LEAGUE is more than a roadmap to success, it is a journey and a live testimony as you are turning the pages, one by one.

MENTORSHIP -133
BY Dr. BAK NGUYEN & COACH MEL

MENTORSHIP, THE POWER OF SHARING is the conversation between a mentor and his apprentice. This is a journey of discovery, of healing, and of empowerment. Power and wisdom don't fade with time, they morph stronger and shapeless if one can renew purpose. Walking legends, writing history, even for seduction, one needs to understand and master the POWER OF MIRRORS to grow, to win. The power of mirrors is the only power that won't corrupt its host. It might blind, but not corrupt. And the only way to avoid blindness in the light of great power is to have a mirror to react to. This is the essence of a mentor/apprentice relationship. To the apprentice, it is the privilege to gain much power and wisdom. To the mentor, it is the chance to break the limits of his or her own power to ascend into even greater power. MENTORSHIP, THE POWER OF SHARING is the conversation between Dr. Bak and Coach Mel, on her path to setting the next world record mark in literature, beating her mentor. It is the universal dynamic of every mentor-apprentice synergy. Welcome to the Alphas.

MIDAS TOUCH -065
POST-COVID DENTISTRY
BY Dr. BAK NGUYEN, Dr. JULIO REYNAFARJE AND Dr. PAUL OUELLETTE

MIDAS TOUCH, is the memoir of what happened in the ALPHAS SUMMIT in the midst of the GREAT PAUSE as great minds throughout the world in the dental field are coming together. As the time of competition is obsolete, the new era of collaboration is blooming. This is the 3rd book of the ALPHAS, after AFTERMATH and RELEVANCY, all written in the midst of confinement. Dr. Julio Reynafarje is bearing this initiative, to share with you the secret of a successful and lasting relationship with your patients, balancing science and psychology, kindness, and professionalism. He personally invited the ALPHAS to join as co-author, Dr. Paul Ouellette, Dr. Paul Dominique, and Dr. Bak. Together, they have more than 100 years of combined experience, wisdom, trade, skills, philosophy, and secrets to share with you to empower you in the rebuilding of the dental profession in the aftermath of COVID. RELEVANCY was about coming together and rebuilding the future. MIDAS TOUCH is about how to build, one treatment plan at a time, one story at a time, one smile at a time.

MINDSET ARMORY -050
BY Dr. BAK NGUYEN

MINDSET ARMORY is Dr. Bak's 49th book, days after he completed his world record of writing 48 books within 24 months, on top of being the CEO of Mdex & Co and a full-time cosmetic dentist. Dr. Bak is undoubtedly an OVERACHIEVER. In his last books, he has shared more and more of his lifestyle and how it forged his winning mindset. Within MINDSET ARMORY, Dr. Bak is sharing with us his tools, how he found them, forged them, and leverage them. Just like any warrior needs a shield, a sword, and a ride, here are Dr. Bak's. For any entrepreneur, the road to success is a long and winding journey. On the way, some will find allies and foes. Some allies will become foes, and some foes might become allies. In today's competitive world, the only constant is change. With the right tool, it is possible to achieve. The right tool, the right mindset. This is MINDSET ARMORY.

MIRROR-085
BY Dr. BAK NGUYEN

MIRROR is the theme for a personal book. Not only to Dr. Bak but to all of us looking to reach beyond who and what we actually are. MIRROR is special in the fact that it is not only the content of the book that is of worth but the process in which Dr. Bak shared his own evolution. To go beyond who we are, one must grow every day. And how do you compare your growth and how far have you reached? Looking in the mirror. In all of Dr. Bak's writing, looking at the past is a trap to avoid at all costs. Looking in the mirror, is that any better? Share Dr. Bak's way to push and keep pushing himself without friction or resistance. Please read that again. To evolve without friction or resistance… that is the source of infinite growth and the unification of the Quest for Power and the Quest of Happiness.

MOMENTUM TRANSFER -009
BY Dr. BAK NGUYEN & Coach DINO MASSON

How to be successful in your business and life? Achieve Your Biggest Goals With MOMENTUM TRANSFER. START THE BUSINESS YOU WANT - AND BRING IT NEXT LEVEL! GET THE LIFE YOU ALWAYS WANTED - AND IMPROVE IT! TAKE ANY PROJECTS YOU HAVE - AND MAKE THEM THE BEST! In this powerful book, you'll discover what a small business owner learnt from a millionaire and successful entrepreneur. He applied his mentor's principles and is explaining them in full detail in this book. The small business owner wrote the book he has always wanted to read and went from the verge of bankruptcy to quadrupling his revenues in less than 9 months and improve his personal life by increasing his energy and bringing back peacefulness. Together, the millionaire and the small business owner are sharing their most valuable business and life lessons with the world. The most powerful book to increase your momentum in your business and your life introduces simple and radical life-changing concepts: Multiply your business revenues by finding the Eye of your Momentum - Increase your energy by building and feeding your own Momentum - How to increase your confidence with these simple steps - How to transfer your new powerful energy into other aspects of your business and life - How to set goals and achieve them (even crush them!)- How to always tap into an effortless and limitless force within you- And much, much more!

P

PLAYBOOK INTRODUCTION -055
BY Dr. BAK NGUYEN

In PLAYBOOK INTRODUCTION, Dr. Bak is open the door to all the newcomers and aspirant entrepreneurs who are looking at where and when to start. Based on questions of two college students wanting to know how to start their entrepreneurial journey, Dr. Bak dives into his experiences to empower the next generation, not about what they should do, but how he, Dr. Bak, would have done it today. This is an important aspect to recognize in the business world, the world has changed since the INFORMATION AGE and the advent of the millenniums into the market. Most matrix and know-how have to be adapted to today's speed and accessibility to the information. We are living at the INFORMATION AGE, this book is the precursor to the ABUNDANCE AGE, at least to those open to embracing the opportunity.

PLAYBOOK INTRODUCTION 2 -056
BY Dr. BAK NGUYEN

In PLAYBOOK INTRODUCTION 2, Dr. Bak continues the journey to welcome the newcomers and aspirant entrepreneurs looking at where and when to start. If the first volume covers the mindset, the second is covering much more in-depth the concept of debt and leverage. This is an important aspect to recognize in the business world, the world has changed since the INFORMATION AGE and the advent of the millenniums into the market. Most matrix and know-how have to be adapted to today's speed and accessibility to the information. We are living at the INFORMATION AGE, this book is the precursor to the ABUNDANCE AGE, at least to those open to embrace the opportunity.

POWER -043
EMOTIONAL INTELLIGENCE
BY Dr. BAK NGUYEN

IN POWER, EMOTIONAL INTELLIGENCE, Dr. Bak is sharing his experiences and secrets leveraging on his EMOTIONAL INTELLIGENCE, a power we all have within. From SYMPATHY, having others opening up to you, to ACTIVE LISTENING, saving you time and energy; from EMPATHY, allowing you to predict the future to INFLUENCE, enabling you to draft the future, not to forget the power of the crowd with MOMENTUM, you are now in possession of power in tune with nature, yourself. It is a unique take on the subject to empower you to find your powers and your destiny. Visionary businessman, and doctor in dentistry, Dr. Bak describes himself as a Dentist by circumstances, a communicator by passion, and an entrepreneur by nature.

POWERPLAY -078
HOW TO BUILD THE PERFECT TEAM
BY Dr. BAK NGUYEN

In POWERPLAY, HOW TO BUILD THE PERFECT TEAM, Dr. Bak is sharing with you his experience, perspective, and mistake travelling the journey of the entrepreneur. A serial entrepreneur himself, he started venture only with a single partner as a team to build companies with a director of human resources and a board of directors. POWERPLAY is not a story, it is the HOW TO build the perfect team, knowing that perfection is a lie. So how can one build a team that will empower his or her vision? How to recruit, how to train, how to retain? Those are all legitimate questions. And all of those won't matter if the first question isn't answered: what is the reason for the team? There is the old way to hire and the new way to recruit. Yes, Human Resources is all about mindset too! This journey is one of introspection, of leadership, and a cheat sheet to build, not only the perfect team but the team that will empower your legacy to the next level.

PROFESSION HEALTH - TOME ONE -005
THE UNCONVENTIONAL QUEST OF HAPPINESS
BY Dr. BAK NGUYEN, Dr. MIRJANA SINDOLIC, Dr. ROBERT DURAND AND COLLABORATORS

Why are health professionals burning out while they give the best of themselves to heal the world? Dr. Bak aims to break the curse of isolation that health professionals face and establish a conversation to start the healing process. PROFESSION HEALTH is the basis of an ongoing discussion and will also serve as an introduction to a study led by Professor Robert Durand, DMD, MSc Science from the University of Montreal, a study co-financed by Mdex and the Federal Government of Canada. Co-writers are Dr. Mirjana Sindolic, Professor Robert Durand, Dr. Jean De Serres, MD and former President of Hema Quebec, Counsel-Minister Luis Maria Kalaff Sanchez, Dr. Miguel Angel Russo, MD, Banker Anthony Siggia, Banker Kyles Yves, and more… This is the first Tome of three, dedicated to helping "WHITE COATS" to heal and to find their happiness.

140

R

MidLife Crisis is a common theme for each of us as we reach the threshold. As a man, as a woman, why is it that half of the marriages end up in recall? If anything else would have half those rates of failure, the lawsuits would be raining. Where are the flaws, the traps? Love is strong and pure, why is marriage not the reflection of that? Those are all hard questions to ask with little or no answers. Dr. Bak is sharing his reflections and findings as he reached himself the WALL OF MARRIAGE. This is a matter that affects all of our lives. It is time for some answers.

THE GREAT PAUSE was a reboot of all the systems of society. Many outdated systems will not make it back. The Dental Industry is a needed one, it has laid on complacency for far too long. In an age where expertise is global and democratized and can be replaced with technologies and artificial intelligence, the REBOOT will force, not just an update, but an operating system replacement and a firmware upgrade. First, they saved their industry with THE ALPHAS INITIATIVE, sharing their knowledge and vision freely to all the world's dental industry. With the OUELLETTE INITIATIVE, they bought some time for all the dental clinics to resume and adjust. The warning has been given, the clock is now ticking. who will prevail and prosper and who will be left behind, outdated and obsolete?

RISING -062
TO WIN MORE THAN YOU ARE AFRAID TO LOSE
BY Dr. BAK NGUYEN

In RISING, TO WIN MORE TAN YOU ARE AFRAID TO LOSE, Dr. Bak is breaking down the strategy to success to all, not only those wearing white coats and scrubs. More than his previous book (SUCCESS IS A CHOICE), this one is covering most of the aspects of getting to the next level, psychologically, socially, and financially. Rising is broken down into three key strategies: Financial Leverage - Compressing time - Always being in control. Presented by MILLION DOLLAR MINDSET, the book is covering more than the ways to create wealth, but also how to reach happiness and live a life without regrets. Dr. Bak the CEO and founder of Mdex & Co, a company with the promise of reforming the whole dental industry for the better. He wrote more than 60 books within 30 months as he is sharing his experiences, secrets, and wisdom.

S

SELFMADE -036
GRATITUDE AND HUMILITY
BY Dr. BAK NGUYEN

This is the story of Dr. Bak, an artist who became a dentist, a dentist who became an Entrepreneur, an Entrepreneur who is seeking to save an entire industry. In his free time, Dr. Bak managed to write 37 books and is a contender for 3 world records to be confirmed. Businessman and visionary, his views and philosophy are ahead of our time. This is his 37th book. In SELFMADE, Dr. Bak is answering the questions most entrepreneurs want to know, the HOWTO and the secret recipes, not just to succeed, but to keep going no matter what! SELFMADE is the perfect read for any entrepreneurs, novices, and veterans.

SHORTCUT vol. 1 - HEALING -093
BY Dr. BAK NGUYEN

In SHORTCUT 408 HEALING QUOTES, Dr. Bak revisits and compiles his journey of healing and growing. Just like anyone, he was moulded and shaped by Conformity and Society to the point of blending and melting. Walking his journey of healing, he rediscovers himself and found his true calling. And once whole with himself and with the Universe, Dr. Bak found his powers. In SHORTCUT 408 HEALING QUOTES, you have a quick and easy way to surf his mindsets and what allowed him to heal, to find back his voice and wings, and to walk his destiny. You too are walking your Quest of Identity. That one is mainly a journey of healing. May you find yours and your powers.

SHORTCUT vol. 2 - GROWING -094
BY Dr. BAK NGUYEN

In SHORTCUT 408 GROWTH QUOTES, Dr. Bak is compiling his library of books about personal growth and self-improvement. More than a motivational book, more than a compilation of knowledge, Dr. Bak is sharing the mindsets upon which he found his power to achieve and to overachieve. We all have our powers, only they were muted and forgotten as we were forged by Conformity and Society. After the healing process, walking your Quest of Identity, the Quest for your growth and God-given power is next to lead you to walk your Destiny.

SHORTCUT vol. 3 - LEADERSHIP -095
BY Dr. BAK NGUYEN

In SHORTCUT 365 LEADERSHIP QUOTES, Dr. Bak is compiling his library of books about leadership and ambition. Yes, the ambition is to find your worth and to make the world a better place for all of us. If the 3rd volume of SHORTCUT is mainly a motivational compilation, it also holds the secrets and mindsets to influence and leadership. If you were looking to walk your legend and impact the world, you are walking a lonely path. You might on your own, but it does not have to be harder than it is. As we all have your unique challenges, the key to victory is often found in the same place, your heart. And here are 365 shortcuts to keep you believing and to attract more people to you as you are growing into a true leader.

SHORTCUT vol. 4 - CONFIDENCE -096
BY Dr. BAK NGUYEN

SHORTCUT 518 CONFIDENCE QUOTES, is the most voluminous compilation of Dr. Bak's quotes. To heal was the first step. To grow and find your powers came next. As you are walking your personal legend, Confidence is both your sword and armour to conquer your Destiny and overcome all of the challenges on your way. In SHORTCUT volume four, Dr. Bak comprises all his mindsets and wisdom to ease your ascension. Confidence is not something one is simply born with, but something to nurture, grow, and master. Some will have the chance to be raised by people empowering Confidence, others will have to heal from Conformity to grow their confidence. It does not matter, only once Confident, can one stand tall and see clearly the horizon.

SHORTCUT vol. 5- SUCCESS -097
BY Dr. BAK NGUYEN

Success is not a destination but a journey and a side effect. While no map can lead you to success, the right mindset will forge your own success, the one without medals nor labels. If you are looking to walk your legend, to be successful is merely the beginning. Actually, being successful is often a side effect of the mindsets and actions that you took, you provoked. In SHORTCUT 317 SUCCESS QUOTES, Dr. Bak is revisiting his journey, breaking down what led him to be successful despite the odds stacked against him. As success is the consequence of mindsets, choices, and actions, it can be duplicated over and over again, one just needs to master the mindsets first.

SHORTCUT vol. 6- POWER -098
BY Dr. BAK NGUYEN

That's the kind of power that you will discover within this journey. Power is a tool, a leverage. Well used, it will lead to great achievements. Misused, it will be your downfall. If a sword sometimes has 2 edges, Power is a sword with no handle and multiple edges. You have been warned. In SHORTCUT 376 POWER QUOTES, Dr. Bak is compiling all the powers he found and mastered walking his own legend. If the first power was Confidence, very quickly, Dr. Bak realized that Confidence was the key to many, many more powers. Where to find them, how to yield them, and how to leverage these powers is the essence of the 6th volume of SHORTCUT.

SHORTCUT vol. 7- HAPPINESS -099
BY Dr. BAK NGUYEN

We were all born happy and then, somehow, we lost our ways and forgot our ways home. Is this the real tragedy behind the lost paradise myth? If we were happy once, we can trust our hearts to find our way home, once more. This is the journey of the 7th volume of the SHORTCUT series. In SHORTCUT 306 HAPPINESS QUOTES, Dr. Bak is revisiting and compiling all the secrets and mindsets leading to happiness. Happiness is not just a destination but a shrine for Confidence and a safe place to regroup, to heal, to grow. We each have our own happiness. What you will learn here is where to find yours and, more importantly, how to leverage you to ease the journey ahead, because happiness is not your final destination. It can be the key to your legend.

SHORTCUT vol. 8- DOCTORS -100
BY Dr. BAK NGUYEN

If healing was the first step to your destiny and powers, there is a science to healing. Those with that science are doctors, the healers of the world. In India, healers are second only to the Gods! In SHORTCUT 170 DOCTOR QUOTES, Dr. Bak is dedicating the 8th volume of the series to his peers, doctors, from all around the world. Doctors too, have to walk their Quest of Identity, to heal from their pain and to walk their legend. Doctors need to heal and rejuvenate to keep healing the world. If healing is their science, in SHORTCUT, they will access the power of leveraging.

SUCCESS IS A CHOICE -060
BLUEPRINTS FOR HEALTH PROFESSIONALS
BY Dr. BAK NGUYEN

In SUCCESS IS A CHOICE, FINANCIAL MILLIONAIRE BLUEPRINTS FOR HEALTH PROFESSIONALS, Dr. Bak is breaking down the strategy to success for all those wearing white coats and scrubs: doctors, dentists, pharmacists, chiropractors, nurses, etc. Success is broken down into three key strategies: Financial Leverage - Compressing time - Always being in control. Presented by MILLION DOLLAR MINDSET, the book is covering more than the ways to create wealth, but also how to reach happiness and live a life without regrets. Dr. Bak is a successful cosmetic dentist with nearly 20 years of experience. He founded Mdex & Co, a company with the promise of reforming the whole dental industry for the better. While doing so, he discovered a passion for writing and for sharing. Multiple times World Record, Dr. Bak is writing a book every 2 weeks for the last 30 months. This is his 60th book, and he is still practicing. How he does it, is what he is sharing with us, SUCCESS, HAPPINESS, and mostly FREEDOM to all Health Professionals.

SYMPHONY OF SKILLS -001
BY Dr. BAK NGUYEN

You will enlighten the world with your potential. I can't wait to see all the differences that you will have in our world. Remember that power comes with responsibility. We can feel in his presence, a genuine force, a depth of energy, confidence, innocence, courage, and intelligence. Bak is always looking for answers, morning and night, he wants to understand the why and the why not. This book is the essence of the man. Dr. Bak is a force of nature who bears proudly his title eHappy. The man never ceases smiling and spreading his good vibe wherever he passes. He is not trapped in the nostalgia of the past nor the satisfaction of the present, he embodies the joy of what's possible, and what's to come. The more we read, the more we share, and we live. That is Bak, he charms us to evolve and to share his points of view, and before we know it, we are walking by his side, a journey we never saw coming.

T

THE 90 DAYS CHALLENGE -061
BY Dr. BAK NGUYEN

THE 90 DAYS CHALLENGE, is Dr. Bak's journey into the unknown. Overachiever writing 2 books a month on average, for the last 30 months, ambitious CEO, Industries' Disruptor, Dr. Bak seems to have success in everything he touches. Everything except the control of his weight. For nearly 20 years, he struggles with an overweight problem. Every time he scored big, he added on a little more weight. Well, this time, he exposes himself out there, in real-time and without filter, accepting the challenge of his brother-in-law, DON VO to lose 45 pounds within 90 days. That's half a pound a day, for three months. He will have to do so while keeping all of his other challenges on track, writing books at a world record pace, leading the dental industry into the new ERA, and keep seeing his patients. Undoubtedly entertaining, this is the journey of an ALPHA who simply won't give up. But this time, nothing is sure.

THE BOOK OF ANGELS -134
BY Dr. BAK NGUYEN & WILLIAM BAK

LEGENDS OF DESTINY, THE BOOK OF ANGELS is the Annals of the Angels of the Legends of Destiny. This book is the origin story and the fate of each of the angels and archangels from this epic fresque. As the worlds are clashing and the Gods are out of control, Ethem, the primal force created the angels to balance the forces of the universe. These are the stories of the guardians of balance, the wings of justice, and the tragedies of power and its corruption. Follow Angel Lord Adrian, Archangel Mikael, Hermes, and Lucifer from their fights to their rise and demise. Follow the adventure of Angels Eto, Ethel, Jardoo; follow the rise of Dark Angels Anak, Felice, or Hesdielle. Choose your faction, Archangel, Angels, Dark Angels, Guild, Phantoms, bionics, or hybrid, you will each time be amazed. Caught between the Gods, the Titans, the demons, the elves, the orcs, the humans, and everything in between, the Angels bear the heavy responsibility of balancing life and creation. These are their legends.

THE BOOK OF LEGENDS -024
BY Dr. BAK NGUYEN & WILLIAM BAK

The Book of Legends vol. 1 is the story behind the world record of Dr. Bak and his son, William Bak. All Dr. Bak had in mind was to keep his promise of writing a book with his son. They ended up writing 8 children's books within a month, scoring a new world record. William is also the youngest author having published in two languages. Those are world records waiting to be confirmed. History will say: to celebrate a first world record (writing 15 books / 15 months), for the love of his son, he will have scored a second world record: to write 8 books within a month! THE BOOK OF LEGENDS vol. 1 This is both a magical journey for both a father and a son looking to connect and find themselves. Join Dr. Bak and William Bak in their journey and their love for Life!

THE BOOK OF LEGENDS 2 -041
BY Dr. BAK NGUYEN & WILLIAM BAK

THE BOOK OF LEGENDS vol. 2 is the sequel of "CINDERELLA" but a true story between a father and his son. Together they have discovered a bond and a way to connect. The first BOOK OF LEGENDS covered the time of the first four books they wrote together within a month. The second BOOK OF LEGENDS is covering what happened after the curtains dropped, and what happened after reality kicked back in. If the first volume was about a fairy tale in vacation time, the second volume is about making it last in real Life. Share their journey and their love of Life!

THE BOOK OF LEGENDS 3 -086
THE END OF THE INNOCENCE AGE
BY Dr. BAK NGUYEN & WILLIAM BAK

THE BOOK OF LEGENDS 3 is a long work extending to almost 3 years. If the shocking duo known as Dr. Bak and prodigy William Bak has marked the imaginary writing world record upon world record, the story is not all pink. After the franchise of the CHICKEN BOOKS, William, now in his pre-teen years, wants to move away from the chicken tales. After 22 chicken books, a break is well deserved. that said, what is next? Both father and son thought that if they could do it once easily, they could do it again! They couldn't be any further from the truth. For 2 years, they were stuck in the quest for their next franchise of books. THE BOOK OF LEGENDS 3 started right around the end of the chicken franchise and would have ended with a failure if the book was to be released on time, the holiday season of that year. It took the duo another year to complete their story to add the last chapters of this book, hoping to end with a happy ending. Unfortunately, not all story ends the way we wish… this is the dark tome of the series, where the imagination got eclipsed. Follow William and Dr. Bak in their fight to keep the magic and connection alive.

THE CONFESSION OF A LAZY OVERACHIEVER -089
REINVENT YOURSELF FROM ANY CRISIS
BY Dr. BAK NGUYEN

In THE CONFESSION OF A LAZY OVERACHIEVER, Dr. Bak is opening up to his new marketing officer, Jamie, fresh out of school. She is young, full of energy, and looking to chill and still have it all. True to his character, Dr. Bak is giving Jamie some leeway to redefine Dr. Bak's brand to her demographic, the Millennials. This journey is about Dr. Bak satisfying the Millennials and answering their true questions in life. A rebel himself, his ambition to change the world started back on campus, some 25 years ago… then, life caught up with him. It took Dr. Bak 20 years to shake down the burdens of life, spread his wings free from Conformity, and start Overachieving. Doctor, CEO, and world record author, here is what Dr. Bak would have loved to know 25 years ago as was still on campus. In a word, this is cheating your way to success and freedom. And yes, it is possible. Success, Money, and Freedom, they all start with a mindset and the awareness of Time. Welcome to the Alphas.

THE ENERGY FORMULA -053
BY Dr. BAK NGUYEN

THE ENERGY FORMULA is a book dedicated to helping each individual to find the means to reach their purpose and goal in Life. Dr. Bak is a philosopher, a strategist, a business, an artist, and a dentist, how does he do all of that? He is doing so while mentoring proteges and leading the modernization of an entire industry. Until now, Momentum and Speed were the powers that he was building on and from. But those powers come from somewhere too. From a guide of our Quest of Identity, he became an ally in everyone's journey for happiness. THE ENERGY FORMULA is the book revealing step by step, the logic of building the right mindset and the way to ABUNDANCE and HAPPINESS, universally. It is not just a HOW TO book, but one that will change your life and guide you to the path of ABUNDANCE.

THE MODERN WOMAN -070
TO HAVE IT HAVE WITH NO SACRIFICE
BY Dr. BAK NGUYEN & Dr. EMILY LETRAN

In THE MODERN WOMAN: TO HAVE IT ALL WITH NO SACRIFICE, Dr. Bak joins forces with Dr. Emily Letran to empower all women to fulfill their desires, goals, and ambition. Both overachievers going against the odds, they are sharing their experience and wisdom to help all women to find confidence and support to redefine their lives. Dr. Emily Letran is a doctor in dentistry, an entrepreneur, author, and CERTIFIED HIGH-PERFORMANCE coach. For an Asian woman, she made it through the norms and the red tapes to find her voice. As she learnt and grew with mentors, today she is sharing her secret with the energy that will motivate all of the female genders to stand for what they deserve. Alpha doctor, Bak is joining his voice and perspective since this is not about gender equality, but about personal empowerment and the quest of Identity of each, man and woman. Once more, Dr. Bak is bringing LEVERAGE and REASON to the new social deal between man and woman. This is not about gender, but about confidence.

THE POWER BEHIND THE ALPHA -008
BY TRANIE VO & Dr. BAK NGUYEN

It's been said by a "great man" that "We are born alone and we die alone." Both men and women proudly repeat those words as wisdom since. I apologize in advance, but what a fat LIE! That's what I learnt and discovered in life since my mind and heart got liberated from the burden of scars and the ladders of society. I can have it all, not all at the same time, but I can have everything I put my mind and heart into. Actually, it is not completely true. I can have most of what I and Tranie put our minds into. Together, when we feel like one, there isn't much out of our reach. If I'm the mind, she's the heart; if I'm the Will, she's the means. Synergy is the core of our power. Tranie's aim is always Happiness. In Tranie's definition of life, there are no justifications, no excuses, no tomorrow. For Tranie, Happiness is measured by the minutes of every single day. This is why she's so strong and can heal people around her. That may also be why she doesn't need to talk much, since talking about the past or the future is, in her mind, dimming down the magic of the present, the Now. We both respect and appreciate that we are the whole balancing each other's equation of life, of love, of success. I was the plus and the minus, then I became the multiplication factor and grew into the exponential. And how is Tranie evolving in all of this? She is and always will be the balance. If anything, she is the equal sign of each equation.

THE POWER OF Dr. -066
THE MODERN TITLE OF NOBILITY
BY Dr. BAK NGUYEN, Dr. PAVEL KRASTEV AND COLLABORATORS

In THE POWER OF Dr., independent thinkers mean to exchange ideas. An idea can be very powerful if supported by a great work ethic. Work ethic, isn't that the main fabric of our white coats, scrubs, and title? In an era post-COVID where everything has been rebooted and that's the healthcare industry is facing its own fate: to evolve or to be replaced, Dr. Bak and Dr. Pavel reveal the source of their power and their playbook to move forward, ahead. The power we all hold is our resilience and discipline. We put that for years at the service of our profession, from a surgical perspective. Now, we can harness that same power to rewrite the rules, the industry, and our future. Post-COVID, the rules are being rewritten, will you be part of the team or left behind? "You can be in control!" More than personal growth and a motivational book, THE POWER OF Dr. is an awakening call to the doctor you look at when you graduate, with hope, with honour, with determination.

THE POWER OF YES -010
VOLUME ONE: IMPACT
BY Dr. BAK NGUYEN

In THE POWER OF YES, Dr. Bak is sharing his journey, opening up and embracing the world, one day at a time, one task at a time, one wish at a time. Far from a dare, saying YES allowed Dr. Bak to rewrite his mindset and break all the boundaries. This book is not one written in a few days or weeks, but the accumulation of a journey for 12 months. The journey started as Dr. Bak said YES to his producer to go on stage and speak... That YES opened a world of possibilities. Dr. Bak embraced each and every one of them. 12 months later, he is celebrating the new world record of writing 9 books written over a period of 12 months. To him, it will be a miss, missing the 12 on 12 mark. To the rest of the world, they just saw the birth of a force of nature, the Alpha force. THE POWER OF YES is comprised of all the introductions of the adult books written by Dr. Bak within the first 12 months. Chapter by chapter, you can walk in his footstep seeing and smelling what he has. This is reality-literature with a twist of POWER. THE POWER OF YES! Discover your potential and your power. This is the POWER OF YES, volume one. Welcome to the Alphas.

THE POWER OF YES 2 -037
VOLUME TWO: SHAPELESS
BY Dr. BAK NGUYEN

In THE POWER OF YES, volume 2, Dr. Bak is continuing his journey, discovering his powers and influence. After 12 months of embracing the world by saying YES, he rose as an emerging force: he's been recognized as an INDUSTRIES DISRUPTOR, got nominated ERNST AND YOUNG ENTREPRENEUR OF THE YEAR, wrote 9 books within 12 months while launching the most ambitious private endeavour to reform his own industry, the dental field. Contender too many WORLD RECORDS, Dr. Bak is doing all of that in parallel. And yes, he is sleeping his nights and yes, he is writing his book himself, from the screen of his iPhone! Far from satisfied, Dr. Bak missed the mark of writing 12 books within 12 months. While everything is taking shape, everything could also crumble down at each turn. Now that Dr. Bak understands his powers, he is looking to test them and push them to their limits, looking to keep scoring world records while materializing his vision and enterprises. This is the awakening of a Force of Nature looking to change the world for the better while having fun sharing. Welcome to the Alphas.

THE POWER OF YES 3 -046
VOLUME THREE: LIMITLESS
BY Dr. BAK NGUYEN

In THE POWER OF YES, volume 3, the journey of Dr. Bak continues where the last volume left, in front of 300 plus people showing up to his first solo event, a Dr. Bak's event. On stage and in this book, Dr. Bak reveals how 12 months of saying YES to everything changed his life… actually, it was 18 months. From a dentist looking to change the world from a dental chair into a multiple times world record author, the journey of openness is a rendezvous with Fate. Dr. Bak is sharing almost in real-time his journey, and experiences, but above all, his feelings, doubts, and comebacks. From one book to the next, from one journey to the next, follow the adventure of a man looking to find his name, his worth, and his place in the world. Doing so, he is touching people Doing so, he is touching people and initiating their rise. Are you ready for more? Are you ready to meet your Fate and Destiny? Welcome to the Alphas.

THE POWER OF YES 4 -087
VOLUME FOUR: RISING
BY Dr. BAK NGUYEN

In THE POWER OF YES, volume 4, the journey continues days after where the last volume left. After setting the new world record of writing 48 books within 24 months, Dr. Bak is not ready to stop. As volume one covers 12 months of journey, volume 2 covers 6 months. Well, volume 3 covers 4 months. The speed is building up and increasing, steadily. This is volume 4, RISING, after breaking the sound barrier. Dr. Bak has reached a state where he is above most resistance and friction, he is now in a universe of his own, discovering his powers as he walks his journeys. This is no fiction story or wishful thinking, THE POWER OF YES is the journey of Dr. Bak, from one world record to the next, from one book to the next. You too can walk your own legend, you just need to listen to your innersole and open up to the opportunity. May you get inspiration from the legendary journey of Dr. Bak and find your own Destiny. Welcome to the Alphas.

THE RISE OF THE UNICORN -038
BY Dr. BAK NGUYEN & Dr. JEAN DE SERRES

In THE RISE OF THE UNICORN, Dr. Bak is joining forces with his friend and mentor, Dr. Jean De Serres. Together both men had many achievements in their respective industries, but the advent of eHappyPedia, THE RISE OF THE UNICORN is a personal project dear to both of them: the QUEST OF HAPPINESS and its empowerment. This book is a special one since you are witnessing the conversation between two entrepreneurs looking to change the world by building unique tools and media. Just like any enterprise, the ride is never a smooth one in the park on a beautiful day. But this is about eHappyPedia, it is about happiness, right? So it will happen and with a smile attached to it! The unique value of this book is that you are sharing the ups and downs of the launch of a Unicorn, not just the glory of the fame, but also the doubts and challenges along the way. May it inspire you on your own journey to success and happiness.

THE RISE OF THE UNICORN 2 -076
eHappyPedia
BY Dr. BAK NGUYEN & Dr. JEAN DE SERRES

This is 2 years after starting the first tome. Dr. Bak's brand is picking up, between the accumulation of records and recognition. eHappyPedia is now hot for a comeback. In THE RISE OF THE UNICORN 2, Dr. Bak is retracing and addressing each of Dr. Jean De Serres' concerns about the weakness of the first version of eHappyPedia and the eHappy movement. This is the sort of creation and a UNICORN both in finance and in psychology. Never before, have you assisted in such a daily and decision-making process of a world phenomenon and of a company. Dr. Bak and Dr. De Serres are literally using the process of writing this series of books to plan and brainstorm the birth of a bluechip. More than an intriguing story, this is the journey of 2 experienced entrepreneurs changing the world.

THE U.A.X STORY -072
THE ULTIMATE AUDIO EXPERIENCE
BY Dr. BAK NGUYEN

This is the story of the ULTIMATE AUDIO EXPERIENCE, U.A.X. Follow Dr. Bak's footsteps in how he invented a new way to read and learn. Dr. Bak brings his experience as a movie producer and a director to elevate the reading experience to another level with entertaining value and make it accessible to everyone, auditive, and visual people alike.

After three years plus of research and development, and countless hours of trials and errors, Dr. Bak finally solved his puzzle: having written more than 1.1 million words. The irony is that he does not like to read, he likes audiobooks! U.A.X. finally allowed the opening of Dr. Bak's entire library to a new genre and media. U.A.X. is the new way to learn and enjoy Audiobooks. Made to be entertaining while keeping the self-educational value of a book, U.A.X. will appeal to both auditive and visual people. U.A.X. is the blockbuster of Audiobooks. The format has already been approved by iTunes, Amazon, Spotify, and all major platforms for global distribution and streaming.

THE VACCINE -077
BY Dr. BAK NGUYEN & WILLIAM BAK

In THE VACCINE, A TALE OF SPIES AND ALIENS, Dr. Bak reprises his role as mentor to William, his 10-year-old son, both as co-author and as doctor. William is living through the COVID war and has accumulated many, many questions. That morning, they got out all at once. From a conversation between father and son, Dr. Bak is making science into words keeping the interest of his son on a Saturday morning in bed. William is not just an audience, he is responsible to map the field with his questions. What started as a morning conversation between father and son, became within the next hour, a great project, their 23rd book together. Learn about the virus, and vaccination while entertaining your kids.

TIMING - TIME MANAGEMENT ON STEROIDS -074
BY Dr. BAK NGUYEN & WILLIAM BAK

In TIMING, TIME MANAGEMENT ON STEROIDS, Dr. Bak is sharing his secret to keep overachieving, and overdelivering while raising the bar higher and higher. We all have 24 hours in a day, so how can some do so much more than others? Dr. Bak is not only sharing his secrets and mindset about time and efficiency, he is literally living his own words as this book is written within his last sprint to set the next world record of writing 100 books within 4 years, with only 31 days to go. With 8 books to write in 31 days, that's a little less than 4 days per book! Share the journey of a man surfing the change and looking to see where is the limit of the human mind, writing. In the meantime, understand his leverage, mindset, and secrets to challenge your own limits and dreams.

TO OVERACHIEVE EVERYTHING BEING LAZY -090
CHEAT YOUR WAY TO SUCCESS
BY Dr. BAK NGUYEN

In TO OVERACHIEVE EVERYTHING BEING LAZY, Dr. Bak retakes his role talking to the millennials, the next generation. If in the first tome of the series LAZY, Dr. Bak addresses the general audience of millennials, especially young women, he is dedicating this tome to the ALPHA amongst the millennials, those aiming for the moon and looking, not only to be happy but to change the world. This is not another take on how to cheat your way to success or how to leverage laziness, but this is the recipe to build overachievers and rainmakers. For the young leaders with ambitions and talent, understanding TIME and ENERGY are crucial from your first steps in writing your our legend. If Dr. Bak had the chance to do it all over again, this is how he would do it! Welcome to the Alphas.

TORNADO -067
FORCE OF CHANGE
BY Dr. BAK NGUYEN

In TORNADO - FORCE OF CHANGE Dr. Bak is writing solo. In the midst of the COVID war, change is not a good intention anymore. Change, constant change has become a new reality, a new norm. From somebody who holds the title of Industries' Disruptor, how does he yield change to stay in control? Well, the changes from the COVID war are constant fear and much loss of individual liberty. Some can endure the change, some will ride it. Dr. Bak is sharing his angle of navigating the changes, yielding the improvisations, and to reinvent the goals, the means to stay relevant. From fighting to keep his companies Dr. Bak went on to let go of the uncontrollable to embrace the opportunity, he reinvented himself to ride the change and create opportunities from an unprecedented crisis. This is the story of a man refusing to kneel and accept defeat, smiling back at faith to find leverage and hope.

TOUCHSTONE -073
LEVERAGING TODAY'S PSYCHOLOGICAL SMOG
BY Dr. BAK NGUYEN & Dr. KEN SEROTA

TOUCHSTONE, LEVERAGING TODAY'S PSYCHOLOGICAL SMOG is mapping to navigate and thrive in today's high and constant stress environment. After 40 years in practice, Dr. Serota is concerned about the evolution of the career of health care professionals and the never-ending level of stress. What is stress, and what are its effects, damages, and symptoms? If COVID-19 revealed to the world that we are fragile, it also revealed most of the broken and the flaws of our system. For now a century, dentistry has been a champion in depression, Drug addiction, and suicide rates, and the curve is far from flattening. Dr. Bak is sharing his perspective and experience dealing with stress and how to leverage it into a constructive force. From the stress of a doctor with no right to failure to the stress of an entrepreneur never knowing the future, Dr. Bak is sharing his way to use stress as leverage.

WHISPER OF DARKNESS -135
BY Dr. BAK NGUYEN & WILLIAM BAK

WHISPER OF DARKNESS is the 3rd volume of LEGENDS OF DESTINY. This time, the story is set at the celestial level, as the war between the angels is raging. After Adrian's ascension to power, the dissident angels left. Some stay isolated as Archangel Anton and Lucifer and will be known as the Errants. Others will regroup and organize. Heaven calls them the Dark Angels, those no more within the light of Heaven. Between the raids to put down the Gods out of control, Heaven is also sending squadrons of Angels to hunt down the dissidents with more or less success. This is the story of angels Ethel and Eto, as they are sent on a recognition mission to uncover the whereabouts of Kohël, a dissident angel, now known as Dali, the God of the Wind. Both junior angels looking to prove their worth to Heaven, the Council of Angels, and their Angel Lord, Adrian. Well, they are not the only ones looking to make their mark, as Hasdielle, a Dark Angel, is also looking to prove Heaven weak and wrong! Follow the legend of Ethel and Eto in WHISPER OF DARKNESS, the 3rd volume of LEGENDS OF DESTINY.

ABOUT THE CO-AUTHORS

From Canada, Dr. BAK NGUYEN is making waves in the dental industry through his company Mdex & Co, his organization, The Alphas, and his books. Dr. Bak has been recognized for his exceptional achievements, including being nominated for the Ernst and Young Entrepreneur of the Year award, receiving the Grand Homage Lys Diversity award, and being named the LinkedIn & TownHall Achiever of the Year and one of the Top 100 Doctors in 2021. His recent accomplishment includes making it to the CREA Global Award list in 2023. He is the first dentist ever to make that list, in 2022, Bill Gates and Sir Richard Branson were part of that list.

In addition to his successful dental career, Dr. Bak is an accomplished author and motivational speaker. He holds several world records for his prolific writing, having written an impressive 120 books in just five years. He has written extensively on topics such as entrepreneurship, leadership, the quest for identity, dentistry and medicine, parenting, children's books, and philosophy. Dr. Bak's passion for sharing knowledge and empowering others led him to establish the international collaborative initiative called THE ALPHAS, aimed at supporting entrepreneurs and doctors during challenging times like the pandemic and economic depression.

Dr. Bak's influence extends beyond his professional endeavours. He co-founded Emotive World Incorporated in 2016, a tech research company focused on utilizing technology to enhance happiness and sharing. Their flagship project, U.A.X., combines the latest advancements in artificial intelligence and techniques from the movie industry to revolutionize the book industry and improve continuing education. By 2023, he is leading the advancement of book writing and audiobook through AI.

With his remarkable achievements, Dr. Nguyen has gained recognition from the international and diplomatic community, sparking global discussions on the well-being and future of the health profession. He actively encourages healthcare professionals to share their experiences and thoughts, emphasizing the importance of unity and collaboration in overcoming challenges.

Dr. Bak's multifaceted persona is described in his own words: a dentist by circumstances, an entrepreneur by nature, and a communicator by passion. His contributions have earned him acknowledgments from the Canadian Parliament and the Canadian Senate, further solidifying his impact and influence.

From Canada, **William Bak**, is a 13 years old prodigy. At the age of 8 years old, he co-wrote a series of chicken books with his dad, Dr. Bak. Together, they are changing the world, one mind at a time, writing books for kids. So far, they have 42 books together and one solo.

He co-wrote the 11 chicken books in ENGLISH and then, had to translate his own books in FRENCH. This is how he has 22 chicken books. William also co-wrote 2 parenting books with his dad, Dr. Bak, the trilogy of THE BOOK OF LEGENDS, THE RISE OF LEGENDS vol.1. 2 Vaccine books (French and English), TIMING, William's first Apollo Protocol book. Lately, William has also written his first book solo at the age of 11, PAPA, J'SUIS PAS CON, HOW TO WRITE 2 BOOKS IN 10 DAYS, and the LEGENDS OF DESTINY, volumes one to four. As well as the trilogy of PAPALAND.

To promote his books, William embraced the stage for the first time in 2019 talking to a crowd of 300+ people. Since he has appeared in many videos to talk about his books and upcoming projects.

In the midst of COVID, he got bored and started his YOUTUBE CHANNEL : GAMEBAK, reviewing video games.
By the end of 2020, he has joined THE ALPHAS as the youngest anchor of the upcoming world project COVIDCONOMICS in which he will give his perspective and host the opinions of his generation.

"I will show you. I won't force you. But I won't wait for you."
- William Bak and Dr. Bak

Writing with his Dad, William holds world records to be officialized:

- The youngest author writing in 2 languages
- Co-author of 8 books within a month
- The first kid to have written 20 children's books
- The child to have written his first solo book in 9 days
- The first child to have co-written 43 books by the age of 13

UAX

ULTIMATE AUDIO EXPERIENCE

A new way to learn and enjoy Audiobooks. Made to be entertaining while keeping the self-educational value of a book, UAX will appeal to both auditive and visual people. UAX is the blockbuster of Audiobooks.

UAX will cover most of Dr. Bak's books and is now negotiating to bring more authors and more titles to the UAX concept. Now streaming on Spotify, Apple Music and Amazon Prime. Available for download on all major music platforms. Give it a try today!

AMAZON - BARNES & NOBLE - APPLE BOOKS - KINDLE
SPOTIFY - APPLE MUSIC

C O M B O

PAPERBACK/AUDIOBOOK

ACTIVATION

Please register your book to receive the link to your audiobook version. Register at:
drbaknguyen.com/lod-whisper-of-darkness-registry

FROM THE SAME AUTHOR
Dr. Bak Nguyen

TITLES AVAILABLE AT

www.Dr.BakNguyen.com

AMAZON - APPLE BOOKS - KINDLE - SPOTIFY - APPLE MUSIC

UNLIMITED ACCESS
DR. BAK'S ENTIRE AUDIO LIBRARY

Since Dr. Bak set his new landmark world record of writing 100 books in 4 years, he is opening his entire audio library, audiobooks and UAX albums, exclusively to all VIP members for $9.99/month.

By becoming a VIP member, you will have access to all Dr. Bak's audiobooks and UAX albums. Those are the ones today bought at Apple Books, Audible, and in COMBO version at Amazon. The UAX albums are those streaming on Apple Music, Spotify, and Amazon Prime Music.

As a VIP, you will also have prime access to the audiobooks as soon as they are completed, hitting them before they reach the mainstream outlets. Get your membership today!

http://drbaknguyen.com/members

Welcome to the Alphas.

www.DrBakNguyen.com

DR.

Bnk Nguyen

www.ingramcontent.com/pod-product-compliance
Lightning Source LLC
Chambersburg PA
CBHW070031260626
47159CB00005B/2010